A SECOND CHANCE FOR THE PILOT'S GIRL

THE PILOT'S GIRL SERIES BOOK 4

FENELLA MILLER

First published in 2020 as Barbara's War The Conclusion. This edition first published in Great Britain in 2024 by Boldwood Books Ltd.

Cover Design by Colin Thomas

Cover Photography: Colin Thomas and Alamy

A CIP catalogue record for this book is available from the British Library.

Paperback ISBN 978-1-83518-653-4

Large Print ISBN 978-1-83518-652-7

Hardback ISBN 978-1-83518-651-0

Ebook ISBN 978-1-83518-654-1

Kindle ISBN 978-1-83518-655-8

Audio CD ISBN 978-1-83518-646-6

MP3 CD ISBN 978-1-83518-647-3

Digital audio download ISBN 978-1-83518-649-7

Boldwood Books Ltd
23 Bowerdean Street
London SW6 3TN
www.boldwoodbooks.com

1

ESSEX, ENGLAND, JANUARY 1944

The Christmas decorations were down and safely in the attic. It was one year and nine months since Alex's return. She rubbed her rounded stomach and smiled. This pregnancy was so much easier than the last as there was no doubt about who was the father.

'Mummy, is the baby coming out yet?' Charlie, an adorable and precocious three-year-old, was eager for his brother or sister to appear.

'Not for a few more weeks, darling, and hopefully Daddy will be able to get leave when your little brother or sister does arrive.'

'I would rather have a brother. Then he can play cricket with me. Tom and David are teaching me how to bowl. I'm going to play cricket for England when I grow up.'

'That's nice, Charlie. Daddy and I can come and watch you play at Lord's cricket ground.'

'No, girls don't watch cricket. Just Grandpa, my uncles and my daddy can come. You and Grandma can stay at home and do girls' things.'

'I see. Did you know that women are delivering the aircraft for the RAF? They can fly the really big planes, like the ones with four engines that flew over the other day. Daddy said one of the ATA girls brought him his new Spitfire a few weeks ago.'

Her son's eyes widened. 'Mummy, it's very naughty to tell me lies. I'm going to play with my train set until teatime. Tom and David will be back soon and will help me finish the new station.'

He ran off and she smiled. Wherever was he getting these old-fashioned ideas from? As far as she was concerned women could do most things a man could do as long as physical strength wasn't involved. If she had a daughter this time, she would make very sure she had as good an education as Charlie was going to get.

Tom would be taking his school certificate soon but would return in the sixth form to take his highers and then hopefully go to Oxford where Grandpa had studied medicine. Her half-brothers had been adopted by her grandparents several years ago and had changed their name to Sinclair. Tom was half a head taller than her and already shaving occasionally. He was a handsome young man, intelligent, kind and funny – and she thanked God every day that he wasn't old enough to be conscripted.

David was a more sensitive soul, less outgoing, and said that he wanted to be a doctor too. His grades were better than Tom's and she was certain he would get into medical school with no difficulty, if that's what he wanted, in a few years' time.

Joe, the housekeeper Mrs Brown's son, had been conscripted last year but so far had remained in England. He had been able to come back on leave several times, much to everyone's delight. Fortunately, both her brothers were now excellent riders and Grandpa had bought a sturdy hunter so they could ride out together. They were also taking care of the horses, dogs, cats and chickens. She was jerked from her musings by Grandma calling up the stairs.

'Barbara, your grandfather has just come home and he's got a tin of real coffee. Are you coming down to have some?'

'I just want to check on Charlie, then I'll be down.'

Her son was happily playing with the train set so she left him to it, knowing he wouldn't require her attention unless something broke or stopped working.

A slight movement behind the rocking horse made her smile. Buttons and Patch, the family dogs, had crept in and were hiding in case they got sent downstairs again. If they were up here then Lavender, Mrs B's huge grey cat, wouldn't be far away. The three were inseparable.

If the animals were with Charlie, when he got bored with his train he'd play with them instead. The telephone rang in the study and as she was closest, she dashed in to pick it up.

'The Grove, Mrs Everton speaking.'

'Babs darling, not got long as I'm on duty in ten minutes but I wanted to speak to you. I'm afraid my weekend pass has been cancelled and I won't be able to see you after all.'

'Alex, it's so good to hear your voice; it's been two weeks since we spoke. Everything's tickety-boo here. Grandpa seems to be enjoying his leisure time and has even taken up playing Bridge again. Charlie keeps asking when the baby's coming and Tom and David are up to their necks in schoolwork.'

'What about my brothers? I haven't got time to ring Mum and Dad and ask them.'

'Jim's decided he doesn't want to be a farmer but has no idea what he's going to do instead. I told him to just get his exams over with and then he's got two years in the sixth form with Tom to come to a decision. Ned's considering the option that he'll take over the farm from your dad when he retires instead. I spoke to Valerie yesterday and she's having another baby in the summer. I don't think I've got any other news to give you.'

'I'm glad that my sister and you are now getting on okay. You haven't mentioned your grandmother – I take it she's in fine form as usual.'

'She isn't going as much to WVS and the WI, which is a concern. She was so involved before.'

Her husband chuckled. 'I expect they'll be glad of the respite. Take care, my darling, and kiss Charlie for me. Keep writing. It makes things a little better being able to read about you when I can't get home.'

'Sometimes I think I'm posting them into a void as I rarely get a reply. I'm glad they mean something to you.'

'I've got a letter half-written and I try and add a bit to it whenever I have time. I think I'll post it to you as it is, just to show that I'm thinking about you all. We're expecting these bombing raids to be the last attempt by Hitler to damage us.'

'I listen every night to the bombers and hate to think of you being up there with them.'

'We're not accompanying our chaps at the moment but concentrating on defence. Thank God not many of the blighters are getting through, but I worry a stray bomb could land on The Grove.'

'Please, don't worry about us. This beastly war's coming to an end. The Germans are almost defeated. Next year things will be different and we can be together again.'

She heard someone telling Alex to get a move on. They hurriedly said goodbye and then the line went dead. Since he'd come back at Easter in 1942 she'd treasured every day she'd been able to spend with him. It had taken him months to regain his strength and be cleared by the medics to return to active duty at his base, Hornchurch.

Initially, as a squadron leader, he'd not been required to fly but last August he was back in a Spitfire and leading his men from the front. Fortunately, the Luftwaffe bombing raids had only resumed in December, which had given him plenty of time to settle back to his role as a fighter pilot.

However, this meant that his squadron had been escorting the English bombers when they flew most nights to destroy the remaining German cities. When the baby blitz began she'd been constantly on edge as his squadron were at the forefront of shooting down the Luftwaffe bombers.

* * *

In the middle of February Alex returned from a busy night of continuous scrambles over France and after stowing his kit in dispersal he made his way to the lorries waiting to take them back to Hornchurch. Night flying was second nature to him now, although he knew that some of his bods still found it difficult flying with instruments alone.

As always the lorry was quieter on the return journey than it had been on the way out as the men were tired and hungry. After the debrief, they would drift to the mess before crashing out. He scratched his two-day ginger stubble and grinned ruefully.

He hadn't had time to shave yesterday and was glad that Babs couldn't see him so dishevelled. Charlie had been born five weeks prematurely in the most appalling circumstances. He wondered if this baby would come early too, but Edward – his grandfather-in-law – had assured him this was unlikely as Charlie's early arrival had been caused by the fact Babs had been in a shelter upon which a house had collapsed.

He yawned, making his jaw crack, and decided he would grab something to eat and then head immediately for his billet. An NCO waylaid him on the way to the debrief.

'Squadron Leader Everton, sir, you've been asked to report to the adjutant immediately.'

Alex's stomach somersaulted. He was almost running by the time he burst into the office. Urgent messages usually heralded bad news of some sort.

'There you are, Alex old son. Don't look so panicked – not bad news at all. Take a pew. This won't take long.'

He sank into the nearest chair facing the adjutant's desk. 'Thank God for that. I thought Babs was in trouble.'

'I'm afraid you're leaving here. They want you to take over a squadron of rocket Typhoons. You'll be based at Holmsley South. It's a large airfield about twelve miles outside Bournemouth, in case you don't recognise the name. You'll be taking over Squadron 245 – the current chappie broke his leg playing silly buggers at the local hostelry.'

For a moment Alex couldn't take in this news. He blinked and rubbed his eyes. 'Rocket Typhoons? Why me? I've never flown one of the blighters.'

'You're the best night flyer on this base, which is why they want you. I'm afraid you don't get any leave. A taxi Anson will be here at midday. That gives you time for a few hours of shut-eye before you leave.'

'I presume I'm getting time to fly one of these so-called fighters before having to be operational?'

'Plenty of time to become accustomed to it before things get hot. Once you're settled and have got to know the kite and your men, you'll not have time to miss us. By the time your baby comes you'll be able to have a few days' leave. It's not due for a bit, is it?'

'No, not until the middle of next month.'

'Good show. You'd better get off, old man. We'll be sorry to lose you but you're needed elsewhere and there's a war on.'

Alex glanced at his watch. Too bloody early to ring Babs and give her the bad news. Bournemouth was about one hundred and fifty miles from his home in Ingatestone – too bloody far to get there and back in a few hours. Babs wasn't going to be happy about this.

The rest of his squadron weren't too happy about his posting either. He shook hands with all of them, wished them luck and then retreated to his quarters. As a senior officer he had his own orderly and decent accommodation.

'I've packed your kit, sir. Clean uniform waiting. If you give me what you're wearing I'll get it washed and back before you leave. Do you want me to collect your flying gear from dispersal?'

'Would you, Alf? That would give me an extra hour's kip. Much appreciated. I'll be sorry to lose your excellent services. I hope the next officer you get appreciates you.'

'Reckon he will. I ain't no mug when it comes to this orderly business.'

* * *

He left ample time to make that all-important phone call to Babs. Elspeth, his grandmother-in-law, answered the telephone. 'Alex, how lovely to hear from you. I'll fetch Babs for you.'

There was a clatter as the receiver was put down on the desk in the study and then he heard the distinctive clip of her heels as she hurried away to find his beloved girl. They'd both believed that what had happened to him would make him exempt from further excitement. Having been shot down, and then been an evader for months, before eventually finding his way back, he'd hoped the War Office would keep him at Hornchurch. Babs picked up the receiver.

'Darling, it's been ages since we spoke. I loved your long letter even if it was only half-finished.'

There was no point in prevaricating. He told her he was being posted and she didn't take it well.

'You said you would be at Hornchurch until the end of the war. Bournemouth is miles away. You'll never get home to see us now.'

'I know, sweetheart. It's rotten luck but I have to go where I'm needed. As soon as I've familiarised myself with the new kite I'll be able to get a few days' leave. As long as there's no big flap on at the time, I'll get compassionate leave when the baby comes and be able to spend a week at home with you all.'

He knew she was crying and it killed him that he couldn't do anything to comfort her. 'I love you, Babs. It will all be over this time next year and we can be together. Please, don't be upset. It's bad for you and the baby.'

They talked for a few minutes more about Charlie and her brothers, and then reluctantly he was forced to end the call as he only had ten minutes left. You had to be there when the taxi rolled to a halt as it wouldn't wait for you.

At midday Alex was waiting on the apron for the Anson to disgorge its passengers and then he clambered in. This was flown by a pretty redhead, a member of the ATA, First Officer Angie Benson. Being fellow redheads, they'd become friends over the past few months.

'Alex, I can't believe after what you've been through that they're posting you away from home. Rotten luck.'

'My wife wasn't too happy about it, especially with the baby due in a few weeks.' He made his way to the rear of the aircraft, stowed his chute and kitbag under the seat, and settled in. The Ansons mainly ferried ATA pilots about the place and there was only one other RAF bloke in the kite with him. The other six seats were occupied by those in the dark blue uniform – he no longer found it strange that there was usually a sprinkling of women. They made excellent pilots, so he'd been told, and some of them were even flying the big buggers, the four-engined bombers.

It was a short hop in a plane and he just hoped he would be

able to snag a lift when Babs needed him in a few weeks' time. There was a car driven by a WAAF waiting to collect him. She saluted smartly and insisted on stowing his kit on the back seat herself.

'I'm to deliver you directly to the CO, sir, but I'll take your belongings to your new billet. Your orderly will deal with them for you.'

'Thank you. Is the officers' accommodation adjacent to the adjutant's office?'

'Everything is adjacent to everything else, sir. You'll have no problem finding your way about.'

The taxi had landed on the far side of the airfield, which meant the driver had to circumnavigate the runways in order to reach the cluster of buildings at the far side. This gave him ample time to look around. The place was in good order as far as he could see. He'd never seen a Rocket Typhoon, even in the air, but he'd heard plenty about them. Initially not much of it complimentary. The Sabre engines kept seizing up and the tails falling off. They were faster but less manoeuvrable than his Spit. They'd made improvements and this fighter-bomber had now found itself a valuable niche.

The kite, it appeared, was the best the RAF had for low-flight interception and making ground attacks on tanks, gun emplacements and ground troops. They had been busy since the weather had improved, bombing guns and columns of troops in France. Things were being prepared for the invasion and he had a sinking feeling that in the next few months he was going to be at the forefront of the battle to win the war.

His new wing co greeted him enthusiastically. 'Glad to see you, Everton. Heard good things about you. I warn you that the Typhoon isn't a sweet little bird like your Spitfire. My squadrons are proving invaluable at the moment. You're going to be busy. We need you fully operational ASAP.'

'Yes, sir, I can't wait to take one up. I'll get myself squared away and then have a go, if that's okay with you? I'm puzzled as to why you couldn't just replace your injured bod with someone here.'

'No one with sufficient experience. Officers of your calibre are like gold dust. You've got the rest of today to familiarise yourself. You can meet the other bods this evening.'

Alex saluted but was just waved away. 'None of that nonsense here, Everton. Just do your job efficiently. That's all I ask. Rank isn't important; excellence is. Most of your squadron are non-commissioned officers. I have two flight lieutenants, a handful of pilot officers and you. Which makes you second-in-command here.'

'I won't let you down.' Alex said this with a confidence he hoped wasn't misplaced. If he was going to be in the thick of it from tomorrow then he'd better get as much airtime as possible.

* * *

An hour later he was sitting in the cockpit for the first time. The Typhoon didn't have the sleek lines of a Spitfire. It was bigger and clumsier. Even getting in was different. He settled into the seat and the strange car-like doors on either side were slammed shut and the lid was dropped down. He wasn't impressed that a member of the ground crew was obliged to reach in and bolt the lid shut.

Did this mean there was no chance of bailing out of this kite? If he went down, he'd likely be cooked alive before anyone could undo the bolt and release him. This didn't fill him with confidence. Little point in having a chute flying in a Typhoon. Then he smiled wryly. He was an idiot. There was an ejection lever to pull and no doubt that released the canopy.

He was used to being in confined spaces. There wasn't much elbow room in the cockpit of any fighter, so the narrow cockpit didn't bother him. He ran through his preflight checks and was ready to take it up.

He had his oxygen mask on and working immediately as fumes from the engine trickled into the cockpit, making it lethal otherwise. Another black mark as far as he was concerned.

As long as he didn't make a complete clot of himself on this first flight he'd be pleased. The kite was a bastard on take-off, but he was ready for the vicious swings. Once airborne he began to enjoy flying something different. He stayed up for an hour, did a few barrel rolls, flew at 10,000 feet and then at treetop level. When he came in to land he was positive he'd not disgraced himself in front of his men.

That night in the mess, he met the squadron he would be leading and they were no different from the chaps he'd left behind. They might have more experience than him flying this fighter-bomber but were happy enough to have him in command.

The only thing that bothered him about this new posting was the fact he was likely to spend more of his time flying over France than he was England. This was a fact he'd keep from Babs.

2

'Babs, it's John on the phone,' Tom called from downstairs.

There was no way on God's earth she could hurry down the stairs now she was so huge. She had another five weeks to go before the baby was delivered – she couldn't wait and hoped that he or she might decide to come before the middle of March.

'I'm coming, Tom, but slowly. Charlie's fast asleep at last.' She negotiated the last few stairs and hoped that in the not too distant future they would be able to use the main staircase again as the blackout would be lifted. The servants' staircase, even with the carpet put down, was too narrow and steep for a woman in her condition.

'Did John say what he wanted? I wonder if he's ringing to tell us when he's getting married to Maggie.'

Her brother pulled a face and shook his head. 'I don't think whatever he's ringing about is good news, Babs.'

Auntie Irene and Uncle Bill – not actual relatives but she'd practically grown up in their kitchen so considered them as family – must be in their sixties now, not really old at all. Her heart was hammering uncomfortably. She almost tipped onto her nose in her hurry to reach the phone. She sent up a hasty prayer to a God she wasn't sure actually existed that the bad news wasn't about either of them.

'John, sorry to keep you waiting but it takes me much longer to get anywhere at the moment.'

'I wanted to tell you myself that Maggie and I have decided we don't suit after all. Mum and Dad are devastated as you might imagine, but I'm not going to marry someone just to please them.'

'I'm so sorry. Alex and I were happy for you. Is there any chance you might have a reconciliation?'

There was silence on the other end of the line for a few moments. 'No, I broke it off. It wasn't fair to marry her when I'm still in love with you.'

She dropped the receiver with a clatter onto the desk in the study, too shocked to answer. She could hear him calling her name but ignored it whilst she gathered her thoughts. After several steadying breaths she retrieved the telephone.

'I'm sorry that you still have feelings for me, John, but I don't know why you felt compelled to tell me. I'm very happily married to Alex. I've never been in love with you and it's time you got over this nonsense.'

'I'm telling you because I'm going to come and see my son. I'm not going to have any other children...'

'You'll do no such thing. Charlie's far too young to know anything about all that. Alex and I told you that when we think he's old enough we'll explain and then he can decide if he wants to get to know you and meet Auntie Irene and Uncle Bill.'

'I don't give a damn about what you and Alex want. Charlie is as much mine as he is yours. Alex has no right to be called his father.'

'As far as everyone's concerned, he's Alex's son. Legally and in every other respect. I thought better of you. This conversation is terminated. Goodbye.'

It took several attempts to get the receiver back in place as her hands were shaking. How could John even think to come here and ruin her family like that? The John she'd known all her life, the man she loved like a brother, was a good man and she didn't understand why he'd behaved the way he had.

She kicked out a chair with her foot and sank into it, fearing her legs would no longer support her weight. The baby was heaving and kicking inside her as if it too was shocked at the change in John. The telephone rang next to her and she almost didn't pick it up, thinking it was probably John again.

'The Grove, Mrs Everton speaking.'

'Babs, love, did John just ring you up?' It was Auntie Irene and she sounded as distressed as Babs was.

'He did. I didn't recognise him. Was he very upset about the engagement being cancelled?'

'No, it's Maggie who is devastated. John told her he was still in love with you and that was the end of it. This past year he's changed. He's not the man he was. He's drinking heavily and is very short-tempered.'

'I'm so sorry to hear that. It's so out of character for him to be drinking like that. I can't believe he still has real feelings for me after all this time. Good heavens, thousands of people have died during this horrible war and their loved ones haven't taken to drink but just got on with it.'

'He shouldn't have rung you; I told him not to. He has nothing to do with you now and I can only apologise. He's not been the same since his accident. He has terrible nightmares and wakes up shouting.'

'It took Alex months to be able to sleep and eat properly so I'm not surprised John's still finding it hard. Has Maggie left now the engagement is off?'

'Yes, they've moved her to another farm, which is only fair. Are you keeping well, Babs love? When's the little one due?'

'Five weeks today and I can't wait. I'm absolutely massive. Now Alex is flying Typhoons and not Spitfires I'm terrified he's going to be shot down again.'

'I thought after what he went through that he'd have a desk job and not be back on active duty like this.'

'He did have a desk job for quite some time but then asked to be flying again and, because they're short of good pilots, they agreed. At least the weather's not too bad for February. Let's hope we don't get any more snow this winter.'

'I'm praying this is the last winter of the war. Uncle Bill says to give you his love. I've got to go now. Goodbye, Babs. Let us know when the baby comes, won't you?'

'I certainly will. And don't worry about John upsetting me; he's obviously not himself.'

They said their goodbyes and she sat for a few moments trying to understand what had just happened. Although she'd agreed that John could tell his parents that Charlie was his child eventually, despite his threats, he'd obviously not done so. Could it be keeping the secret that was making him so unlike himself?

After the dreadful crash that he'd been lucky to survive, he'd been absolutely fine apart from his hideously mangled leg. She'd have to speak to Grandpa and see if he could throw any light on it. He hadn't been a practising doctor for a couple of years but he would still have all the knowledge she needed.

If she didn't get a move on Grandma would come and look for her and she didn't wish to involve them in this. Grandpa had been looking frailer recently and she feared that he was about to have another heart attack. He'd made a full recovery from the one he'd had two years ago but he was in his early seventies and one must expect things to go wrong at that age.

The delicious aroma of freshly made coffee welcomed her into the kitchen. Mrs B, officially the housekeeper but much more than that now, greeted her with a friendly smile.

'I'm taking the tray into the sitting room. You run along and join everyone. I'll keep an ear out for the little one. Mind you, he's quite capable of getting himself downstairs if he wants something. I suppose my Lavvy and those dogs are upstairs with him.'

'They are. Are you sure there's nothing I can take through for you?'

'You don't want to be carrying a tray, not the size you are.'

* * *

Alex acquitted himself well and within a few days was as comfortable flying a Typhoon as he had been a Spitfire. There were regular sorties and he was soon adept at searching out German gun emplacements and blowing them up with the rockets. Things calmed down by the end of February and he asked for a five-day pass.

'As a matter of fact, old boy, I prefer you to go now whilst things are quiet. Doubt you'll get compassionate leave when the baby comes so better to go now.'

'Thank you, sir, much appreciated. If there's a flap on I can be back in a few hours – quicker if I can get a lift to Hornchurch. There's usually a taxi Anson or a Tiger Moth that's coming this way.'

'Let's hope I don't need to call you back.' The adjutant signed and stamped his pass. There was a seat on a taxi in an hour, which gave him ample time to collect his overnight bag. The weather had remained unseasonably warm for the end of

February – none of the heavy snow they'd had previous winters.

Last time he'd spoken to Babs she'd been tearful and begged him to come home immediately even though it meant he wouldn't be able to see the new arrival until he or she was a few weeks old. He was lucky he wasn't stationed overseas; those poor buggers hadn't been home for years. Any children they had would have forgotten them by the time they were demobbed.

The short flip to Hornchurch got him there by lunchtime. He managed to get a lift from a passing army lorry to the station. The second part of his journey was a fraction of the distance but took almost as long to accomplish as the trains were infrequent.

He disembarked at Ingatestone, turned up the collar of his greatcoat, and set off at a brisk walk. He'd not told Babs he was coming today just in case his leave was cancelled at the last minute. It was almost dark when he trudged up the long drive to The Grove. The faint glimmer of his torch was sufficient for him to find his way to the back door. Nobody used the front.

The dogs heard him and were barking noisily behind the door as he opened it. He bent down to fuss them. A small body hurtled from the sitting room and flung himself into his arms.

'Daddy, Daddy, you've come home to see us. Mummy's about to burst.'

He swept his son up in his arms and kissed him. 'I've missed you, Charlie Bear. I hope you've been a good boy.'

He was expecting Babs to come out to greet him and was concerned that she didn't. 'Is your mummy here?'

'Grandpa told her to go to bed. Tom and David are staying with Jim and Ned. Grandpa's upstairs with Mummy and I don't know where my grandma is.'

The housekeeper, Mrs B, appeared in the passageway. 'We didn't know you were coming, Squadron Leader Everton, but Mrs

Everton will be ever so happy to see you. I'm keeping an eye on Sonny Jim as the doctor said your wife needed to rest.'

'I've not eaten since breakfast – can you rustle up something for me, please?' He put his son down and quickly removed his coat.

'Carry me, Daddy. I need a carry.'

Charlie refused to be detached so he bounded up the stairs with his son still in his arms. He had a bad feeling about this and was glad he'd insisted on taking his leave now.

He shouldered open the door to their bedroom and found Edward sitting beside Babs who was actually in bed and not just resting on top of it. His grandfather-in-law scrambled to his feet and his wife's face lit up.

'Alex, I'm so pleased to see you. Don't look so worried, darling – there's nothing wrong with me or the baby. Grandpa just thought it advisable for me to rest a bit more.'

He was across in two strides, dumped Charlie unceremoniously on the floor ignoring his loud protests, and joined Babs on the bed. It was impossible to put his arms around her comfortably but somehow he managed to gather her close. Despite her size, to him she was still the most desirable woman in the world.

They were both breathless when he eventually raised his head. They were alone. Good for Grandpa. He couldn't hear Charlie wailing so he must have been happy to go.

'How long can you stay, Alex?'

'I've got five days but it took most of the first one to get here. I don't remember you being so big or so tired last time. Are you quite sure there's nothing wrong?'

'Grandpa thought for a while that I might be carrying twins but he's certain I'm not. He thinks I've just got a lot of water but also that it's a big baby. He thinks it could come any day. Wouldn't it be wonderful if the baby decided to put in an appearance whilst you're here?'

'Do you have to stay in bed until the baby comes?'

'No, of course not. Grandpa just said to go to bed early but I'm carrying on as usual the rest of the time.'

He kissed her, hard, one last time and then reluctantly rolled from the bed. 'Mrs B is getting me something to eat. I'll put Charlie to bed afterwards and then join you here. Do you want anything from the kitchen?'

'No, not at the moment but a lovely mug of cocoa later on would be wonderful.'

Charlie took some time to settle and he wasn't able to return to Babs until eight o'clock. She was already asleep with only the small table lamp beside the bed switched on. He chucked his clothes on a chair and slid in beside her.

She was as naked as he and before she'd been wearing a voluminous flannel nightie. His pulse quickened. He put his arms around her and she sighed and snuggled backwards. His fingers splayed over the massive bulge of her stomach and a few seconds later the baby began to move. He was amazed she could sleep through the activity. The pressure against his palms was firm. He wasn't sure if it was elbows, knees or feet he was feeling but the baby was obviously healthy and active.

His desire faded and he drifted off to sleep. He was woken by her taking his hands and placing them over her breasts.

'Are you quite sure we should attempt this, darling?'

'The midwife told me making love is an excellent way to bring on labour. Who am I to disagree with an expert?' She giggled. 'Unfortunately, she didn't explain exactly how this could be achieved.'

A highly enjoyable half an hour later they relaxed, satisfied and happy. This was a bonus he hadn't expected on his return. 'Hats off to the midwife, sweetheart. Let's get some sleep and then do it again before Charlie wakes up.'

'That would be absolutely spiffing! Goodnight, darling Alex.'

It was still dark when he was instantly alert. Something was wrong. For a moment he didn't know what it was but then realised the bed was wet. Gently he woke Babs.

'Darling, I think your waters have broken unless you've wet the bed.'

'I haven't had any contractions but I've definitely not peed myself. Please can you put the light on and hand me my nightdress? I think you'd better get dressed before you fetch Grandpa.'

He was halfway to the door and laughed. He tossed her the nightie and then flung on his clothes. By the time he was ready she was on her feet, the blankets tossed back, viewing the large wet stain on the sheet.

'The midwife suggested I put a rubber sheet on the bed and I'm so glad I did. I don't think there's any urgency to fetch anyone, Alex, so will you help me change the sheets?'

'I'll do no such thing. You sit down on a towel and I'll do it on my own. I know where the sheets are kept.'

Twenty minutes later she was back in bed, still no pains, and he was knocking on Edward's door. A sleepy voice answered from inside. 'I'll be there in a minute, Alex. Elspeth is going to get up too as I expect we could all do with a hot drink.'

* * *

Babs wasn't sure if she should be walking about or remain where she was. There'd been no sign of blood or anything else in the wet stain and it definitely hadn't been pee. She found one of the maternity pads and the uncomfortable belt that went with it. This should stop her wetting the bed a second time. Why wasn't she getting contractions? The baby's head had been engaged for the past week and after the flurry of activity earlier was now quiet and she was sure he or she was asleep.

Everything was ready for this delivery; the crib had been scrubbed and the mattress and bedding laundered. The layette, mostly the things that she'd used for Charlie, was waiting in the chest of drawers. The old pram she'd used before had also been cleaned and was already in the boot room.

She wasn't worried. No two deliveries were the same and last time she'd delivered the baby on her own in an Anderson shelter whilst buried beneath the rubble of a house. This should be a piece of cake, as Alex often said, compared to that.

It was odd that she didn't even have a backache and yet her waters had quite definitely broken. She wasn't sure what this meant but Grandpa would be here in a minute to explain and reassure her.

She heard Grandma hurrying downstairs, no doubt to put the kettle on. Then Alex and Grandpa came in. He was carrying his medical bag.

'It's not uncommon for this to happen, my dear, and labour usually starts within twenty-four hours. If you don't mind, I'll just listen to the heartbeat. Has baby been moving about normally?'

'Absolutely, but is sleeping now.'

Grandpa examined her and then smiled. 'Good strong heart-beat – nothing to worry about. Try and get some sleep both of you. No need to ring the midwife yet. Elspeth is making tea. Alex, come with me and collect it.'

The rattle of crockery on a tray announced his return. Alex hadn't brought her any cocoa earlier and she rather hoped it was that and not tea.

'Cocoa and cake for both of us.' He stripped off but this time kept on his underpants. He saw her looking and grinned. 'I had to tell him and he said no more sex now your waters have broken. He was adamant it had nothing to do with what happened.'

She was pink from head to toe at the thought of him discussing something so personal with her grandfather. 'That's a shame. We'll have to wait now until at least six weeks after the baby's born.'

She finished the midnight snack and then decided to tell him about John.

3

Alex listened to Babs and she was obviously far more worried about this development with John than he was. 'He's a good bloke. I'm sure he won't come charging up here to make things difficult for us. He was upset about his broken engagement and taking it out on you.

'I've heard about chaps who've had similar prangs, been lucky not to have gone for a Burton, and are perfectly fine. Months later they become aggressive, unstable and the medics say it's something to do with the trauma and that it affects their brain.'

'I was surprised that he didn't tell Auntie Irene and Uncle Bill that they had a grandchild but I'm glad he didn't. Time enough to involve them when Charlie's old enough to understand. Mind you, the more I think about it the less happy I am at the thought of telling him that his mother was little better than a trollop.'

'For God's sake, don't talk such nonsense. You were engaged to John when you slept with him...'

'Which makes it so much worse that I then did the same with you two weeks later. I hope we never have to tell anyone else.'

He kissed her. 'Forget about it, sweetheart. I have. I don't care whether we have a boy or a girl this time but I would like to see a red-headed little chap running about one day.'

'We haven't really talked about names – do you have any preferences? I suppose we need to make a decision as this baby is going to be here in the next day or two.'

'What about Julia for a girl and Hugh for a boy? As far as I know there are neither of those on either side of the family.'

'I like both of them. I suppose we need a middle name. Julia Elspeth and Hugh Alexander sound perfect.'

'Then we're agreed. When we have other children, and I really would like several more if you're willing, we can use my mum and dad's names.'

He found it hard to settle. Every time she moved he was awake in case she needed him. He'd learnt to sleep whilst waiting to be scrambled. All flyers snatched whatever rest they could in between sorties. This was different – this was something he couldn't control, happening to the woman he loved. Eventually, he dozed off but was up a few hours later, leaving her to sleep, and went in to their son who was banging about in his bedroom.

'What's all the racket, Charlie? Mummy's asleep.'

'I've been chasing Patch and Buttons, Daddy. They're hiding under my bed.' The little boy dropped to his knees and lifted the edge of the bedspread. 'See, naughty doggies.'

'They are bad boys. Let's get you dressed and then we can go and let them out. I expect Mummy would like a nice cup of tea. Do you want to help me make it?'

He snapped his fingers and the dogs crept out on their bellies wagging their tails. They didn't need to be told to leave the bedroom; they scampered out and he could hear their claws on the boards outside.

Mrs B was busy making bread in the kitchen. She already had a tray ready for the oldies and for himself and Babs. 'I'll take both of these up for you. Can you keep an eye on Charlie for a bit? I've told him to let the dogs out.'

He knocked on Edward and Elspeth's door and put the tray down outside. Edward called out that he would come and fetch it and asked how Babs was.

'She's asleep. I'm just going to take up her tea.'

When he walked into their bedroom it was empty and he could hear her moving about in the bathroom. He ran his fingers over his bristly chin. He needed a shave. He'd hated having a beard whilst he'd been imprisoned in the Spanish concentration camp for months.

'Babs, your tea's here.'

'I'll be out in a minute. I'm absolutely fine in case you're wondering.'

'No pains yet?'

'A bit of backache, which I think is the start of labour, but nothing to worry about.'

Whilst she got dressed he used the bathroom, excited at the thought that possibly, later today, he would have another son or a daughter.

Edward knocked on the door as they were about to head downstairs. 'Good show, I think it better for mothers in labour to keep active for as long as possible. However, I don't want you going up and down stairs more than necessary. Feet up on the sofa in the sitting room, my girl. Is that clear?'

Babs smiled. 'Absolutely, Grandpa. I've not had any contractions but I do have backache. The last thing I want to do is rush about.'

'How long have you had the backache?'

'On and off all night, but it's continuous now.'

'In which case, back on the bed and I'd better examine you. Don't want to take any chances. I want the midwife here in good time – I'm too old to deliver a baby.'

Alex remained in the room but tactfully looked away whilst Edward rummaged about underneath Babs's skirts. 'Right, stay where you are, my dear. I need to make a phone call. Things are moving along more swiftly than you realised. Stay on the bed.' He snatched up two pillows and pushed them under her knees. 'Remain like this – it will help.'

He sounded calm and smiled reassuringly but Alex knew at once there was something wrong. He waited until they were outside and heading down the stairs before he spoke.

'What's wrong? Don't fob me off – I know you're worried.'

'She's bleeding. I'm going to call for an ambulance.'

'What does that mean?'

Edward waved him away and snatched up the phone. Alex remained rigid in the doorway listening. He heard the words caesarean section and blood transfusion and knew things were even worse than he'd feared.

'Now, young man, under no circumstances must you let Babs know that both she and the baby are at risk. She needs to remain calm. That will help get much-needed oxygen to the baby.'

'How long will the ambulance be? How long do we have?'

'If the bleeding gets worse then we could lose both of them. The ambulance will be here in fifteen minutes. I'm going to get Elspeth up; you get a bag packed for Babs.'

It took him a few moments to pull himself together. 'Edward, if it's a choice then they must save Babs.'

'Goes without saying, my boy. Hope it won't come to that.'

He walked into the room hoping his smile looked genuine. 'Grandpa's sent for an ambulance. In the circumstances he thinks it better that you deliver in hospital.'

'I thought it was something like that. The baby's been moving as usual, so I'm certain there's nothing wrong with her.'

'You think it's a girl?' He strolled across and dropped down beside her on the bed before putting his hand on the bump. 'Good morning, Julia Elspeth Everton. I can't wait to meet you.'

'You don't mind if it's not a boy this time?'

'I've already got a son, so a daughter will be absolutely perfect.'

'I've got two bags packed; the midwife told me to prepare for every eventuality. They are both in the closet. One with things for the baby, the other for me.'

'That's a relief. I expect I'd have put the wrong things in. Do you think we should tell Charlie or will that upset him?'

'Better not – Grandma can just tell him that his mummy's gone to have the baby and his daddy's gone with her. I hope I don't have to stay in for the full two weeks as I was supposed to have a home delivery.'

'I'll stay with you until I have to return to the base. Good God – do you realise it's the 29th February today? The baby will only have a birthday every four years.'

'I wonder if we can persuade them to put the birth down as either the 28th or March 1st.'

'Despite your grandfather wanting you in hospital immediately the baby might not actually come until tomorrow anyway.'

Every minute dragged. He couldn't keep looking at his watch as that would raise alarm bells. Where was the bloody ambulance? Babs looked as beautiful as ever – he prayed that Edward was being overcautious. If anything happened to her it would destroy him. He could live without any more babies but he couldn't live without her.

The clang of the bell outside heralded the arrival of the ambulance. Now he looked at his watch and it had made excellent time – it had been the longest fifteen minutes of his life. With a minimum of fuss she was transferred to the stretcher, wrapped warmly in red blankets, and carried down the main staircase and out of the front door.

He jumped in with the bags and sat beside her. Edward had said he was going to borrow a car from someone and meet them at Warley Hospital in Brentwood as soon as he could.

* * *

Racing through the countryside with the ambulance bell clanging wasn't a pleasant experience. Babs clutched Alex's hand. 'I don't think they need to go quite so fast. This can't be good for either of us.'

'I think they all travel at this speed. I don't suppose they've got many vehicles available so they always have to hurry so they're available for the next call.'

'Warley Hospital used to be a lunatic asylum, you know? I remember reading about it somewhere.'

'A lot of our bods have gone there when they've had a prang. Nothing but praise for the place. We're slowing down. I think we must be almost there.'

The doors at the back opened and there were nurses waiting to receive her. For the first time, as she was being transferred to the trolley, a flicker of worry passed through her.

She had no time to speak to Alex as she was trundled away at speed. She wasn't taken to the maternity wing but into a cold, tiled room full of frightening medical instruments. A doctor examined her, listened to the baby's heartbeat and then stepped back.

'What's happening? Why am I here?'

The nurses were deftly removing her clothes and replacing them with a surgical gown. The doctor was beside her again. 'Mrs Everton, we need to do a caesarean section immediately. The baby's in distress.'

'Does my husband know?'

'Yes, he's fully aware of the circumstances. Now, try and relax and let us get on with our jobs.'

Needles were stabbed into her hands, lines attached and then a horrible rubber mask was put over her face and she was told to count back from ten.

* * *

Alex paced up and down outside the operating theatre. He wasn't even sure he believed in God, but just in case, he sent up a string of fervent prayers. Why were they taking so bloody long? It had been over an hour and still no one had come out to speak to him.

Edward joined him eventually. 'She is in the best possible hands, my boy. There's nothing you can do but wait.'

'How much longer do you think it'll be?'

'It depends on all sorts of things. The baby will have been delivered some time ago. They will be doing whatever is necessary for Babs now. It depends on what caused the bleeding.'

'Then why don't they bloody well come out and tell me if I've got a son or daughter? Do you think the baby died? Is that why they haven't come out?'

'An infant born by caesarean sometimes has to be kept under close observation for the first twenty-four hours. Sit down, Alex. Prowling up and down isn't doing either of us any good.'

Two hours after they'd taken her into theatre the surgeon emerged. Alex couldn't tell from looking at him if the man was bringing the worst possible news.

'Squadron Leader Everton, you have a healthy daughter. However, Mrs Everton is critically ill. She lost a lot of blood and is being transfused and in the next twenty-four hours things could go either way.'

Alex slumped against the wall. For the past hour he'd feared that he'd lost both of them. He was incapable of speech but Edward took over. He talked quietly to the medic before coming over to explain what was going on.

'I'm sorry, my boy, but at least our Babs is still with us. She's a fighter. She'll pull through this. Unfortunately, the placenta had grown into the wall of her womb, which was causing the haemorrhaging. They had to perform a hysterectomy in order to save her life.'

'Hysterectomy? They've taken out her womb? She'll be devastated that she can't have any more children.'

'You've got two – a boy and a girl. I think on balance she'll be happy enough once she's got used to the idea. She is in recovery but you'll be able to sit with her when she's moved. A nurse is coming to take you to see your baby.'

'Julia Elspeth – we decided on the name last night.'

'Splendid choice. Look, they've come for you now. I'll be here if there's news about Babs. Go and see your daughter.'

Alex followed the nurse through the hospital to the maternity wing and was told to wait in an anteroom. The sweet, sickly smell that he associated with newborns was all-pervasive. Babs wouldn't be able to breastfeed. Another thing she would be upset about. He pushed the thought that she might not live to know about it firmly to the back of his mind.

A different nurse, presumably a midwife of some sort, appeared with a bundle and a beaming smile. 'Here you are, Squadron Leader. She's a lovely little girl. She's got your hair – no mistaking her daddy. Her breathing is excellent. As soon as Mrs Everton is well enough the baby can be with her.'

Alex decided he'd be better off sitting. He didn't want to drop this precious bundle. He cradled her against his arm and pushed the blanket aside to see her face. Despite the dreadful circumstances his mouth curved. He ran his fingers through the downy red hair and his eyes filled. He'd never have a son who looked like him but he had a beautiful daughter who was his image.

The baby gripped his finger when he offered it to her. 'Hello, little one. Mummy isn't too well at the moment but your daddy's here. Your big brother will be thrilled to meet you.'

He lifted the swaddled baby and rested her against his shoulder so he could inhale her baby scent. His connection was total, irrevocable and he understood that he was going to have to be careful not to favour his daughter. Charlie was going to find it hard enough sharing Babs. He was such an intelligent little boy that he was bound to notice Julia was the image of his daddy but he looked like neither of them.

Holding the baby was exactly what he needed. When the nurse came to retrieve her, he felt stronger, more able to face the next few days. Babs would get better. The alternative was too awful to contemplate. One thing he knew was that even if all hell broke loose, he wasn't leaving until his beloved girl was off the danger list. He was quite prepared to be AWOL if necessary.

Later that day he was allowed into a side room where Babs was being taken care of. She had various tubes attached, blood dripping into her arm, and an oxygen mask dangling beside the bed. The sister in charge of critically ill patients spoke quietly to him.

'We are having a comfortable chair brought in for you, Squadron Leader, so you can sleep with some degree of comfort. We'll also supply you with blankets. Your wife is holding her own, but she's still critically ill.'

'Thank you. I saw our daughter. I want to have the baby in here as soon as possible. I think it will help bring my wife back to me.'

'I'll speak to the paediatric consultant. If he agrees that Baby Everton is at no risk then she can be brought in here for a few hours each day.'

'Her name's Julia. Julia Everton – not Baby Everton.' For some reason this seemed important.

The sister didn't answer. He regretted snapping at her but before he could apologise, she was gone in a rustle of starched apron and crisp blue cotton.

* * *

Babs drifted in and out of consciousness and knew something was dreadfully wrong. The second time she came round Alex put a baby in her arms. She was too woozy to ask if it was a girl or a boy but she could see it had glorious russet hair like him. Knowing the baby was healthy, that Alex was here at her side, was enough to allow her to drift back to sleep.

She wasn't sure how long she'd been out of it but when she opened her eyes this time her head was clearer. The room was almost dark, the blackouts down, lit only by a dim orange bulb in the centre of the room. Slowly she turned her head and saw him sprawled in a chair next to her bed fast asleep.

His eyes opened and he was on his feet and beside her instantly. 'Darling Babs, you're back. How do you feel?'

'My tummy's very painful, but apart from that I don't feel too bad. I remember you showing me the baby. Do we have a daughter or a son?'

'Just a minute. You can see for yourself.'

There was a slight squeak of wheels and then a small cot appeared at her side. Even as ill as she was, she was sure the baby should be in the nursery and not in here with them.

'Here you are, sweetheart. Meet Julia Elspeth Everton.'

4

Babs found it difficult to hold the baby but was determined to cuddle her new daughter. Alex kept his hands firmly around the bundle, making sure the weight wasn't on her tummy.

'She looks just like you, darling. I didn't know that babies arrived with such red hair. What's she doing in here with us? Shouldn't she be in the nursery with the other babies?'

'I've been fetching her after everyone's asleep and then taking her back in time for her next feed. I'm sure they know, but no one's said anything.'

'Have I been out of it for long?'

'This is the fourth day. It was touch and go, but I knew you'd pull through. We can't live without you.'

There was something about this statement that bothered her. 'Alex, shouldn't you be back on your base by now? Are you likely to be arrested for still being here?'

'I told the CO I wasn't returning until you were in the clear. He was very understanding, thank God. I'll have to go later today, but you've a string of people waiting to come and see you.'

'What happened? It's all a bit of a blur.'

'You haemorrhaged – but you're on the mend now. You're going to have to stay in here for another couple of weeks, but Edward had you moved into this side room so you'll be able to have visitors as often as you want. Elspeth is going to bring Charlie when you're up to it.'

'Please put Julia back in her crib and then return her to the nursery. I'm not comfortable with having her in here. Is this room on the maternity wing or in the main hospital?'

'Maternity – once you're on your feet you'll be able to move into a ward if you want to be with the other mothers and babies.'

'I'm quite happy where I am, especially if it means I can have visitors whenever I like. If you see a nurse could you ask them if I can have a cup of tea and some toast?'

He vanished with their daughter and she almost called him back. Asking him to find her a cup of tea and some toast had been silly as it was the middle of the night.

The door had been left ajar and the delicious smell of hot toast drifted in. If she sat up a little she would be able to enjoy her midnight feast more. There was no longer a blood transfusion dripping into her arm, which meant she could use both hands to press into the bed and try and wriggle backwards.

Any sort of movement was horribly painful. She didn't dare risk a glance under the sheets to see how bad things were. If her incision looked as awful as it felt then she was horribly mutilated. If she wanted to get better, to get home to Charlie, then she needed to make an effort. She gritted her teeth and somehow managed to sit upright.

A staff nurse came in to take her temperature and blood pressure. 'You gave us a bit of a scare, Mrs Everton, but everything is tickety-boo now. Unfortunately, your milk didn't come in so you won't be able to breastfeed your baby. Mind you, she's doing very well on formula.'

'I don't think I could breastfeed anyway with the way I feel at the moment, so it's a good thing I can't as now I won't feel guilty. Is that toast I can smell?'

'It certainly is. A student nurse is making it and your husband will bring it along on a tray. He's been beside you every minute. Such a lovely man.' She handed Babs two tablets and a glass of water to take them. 'These are painkillers. You'll feel much better when they start to work.'

The nurse bustled off leaving blissful silence behind. Babs had meant to ask exactly what had happened, why she'd been so desperately ill, but didn't have the energy.

'Here you are, sweetheart, we've made enough for both of us as I can't remember the last time I ate. I haven't shaved for four days. I'm surprised you didn't comment.'

'To be honest, I've only just noticed. You do look like a pirate, but a very handsome one.'

The tea was hot, strong and sweet – not how she liked it at all – but it still tasted delicious. The toast and marmalade were even better and between them they polished off all eight slices. She felt considerably better after that. Alex collected up the crockery, brushed every crumb from the bed and side table, and returned it to the small kitchen somewhere along the corridor. He was gone for ages.

'I'm sorry I was so long. I had to use the bog. I also rang your grandparents and told them you're out of danger and they can come visit tomorrow.'

'They must have been terrified when the phone rang in the middle of the night. You should have left it until morning.'

'It's five o'clock – officially morning even though it's pitch-dark outside.'

He kicked off his shoes and carefully lay down beside her so she could rest her head on his shoulder. 'Alex, why am I in such dreadful pain? I'm sure I've never heard anyone say that having a caesarean section is so horrible.'

'There's something I need to tell you, darling, and I know you're going to be upset.'

She listened as he told her why things had gone so disastrously wrong and that the only way to save her life had been to remove her womb. The news was hard to take.

'I'm only twenty-three years old and now have the body of an old woman. You'll never have a son of your own.'

'I've got a son and now I've got a daughter. I'm just thankful I've still got you. Go to sleep, darling. Things won't seem so bleak tomorrow.'

* * *

In fact, things were far worse. Alex left her and she didn't know when she'd see him again. Having his baby was supposed to be the most wonderful thing in the world, but instead it had turned into a nightmare. They brought Julia in so she could give her a bottle but she sent them away. The baby didn't need her – anyone could feed the baby and having the weight on her tummy was just too uncomfortable.

The days drifted past and slowly she regained her strength and, just over two weeks after arriving, she was ready to go home. Charlie had refused to come to the hospital more than once and she was desperate to see him.

The last three days she had been the one feeding Julia. She didn't understand why she was so uninterested in her daughter. It had been instant love when Charlie was born but for some reason this time her maternal instincts just weren't there. Julia could be anybody's baby – Babs just didn't feel she was hers but this was probably to do with how ill she'd been.

Once she was home she was sure things would click into place and she would come to love this little red-headed scrap of humanity.

* * *

Alex hated to leave Babs when she was so poorly but had no option. He'd already been two days over his allotted leave and needed to be back leading his men. Edward had brought his bag into the hospital on the third day so he was able to depart from the hospital in Brentwood.

There had been bombing over the capital since the beginning of the year and he wished he hadn't been transferred. His old squadron were no longer short of experienced pilots and the hole he'd left would soon have been filled by someone else.

He sometimes wondered if the other blokes who'd been evaders with him were now back with their squadrons. The chances of him meeting any of them again were slim but when this damned war was over, he intended to seek them out.

By the time he arrived at the base as it was dark. He scarcely had time to dump his gear before being called into the ops room with the other bods.

'The Huns have been flying in low these past few nights. You chaps are to skip across the channel and shoot them down before they get here. The first wave will leave at four.' He pointed to the map pinned to the board on the wall. 'Details on there. I'll leave you to peruse them.'

The wing commander was a man of few words but tonight his briefing was almost non-existent. Their commanding officer strode out leaving twenty-four rather confused flyers behind.

'Tell me, how many of you have any experience of night fighting?' Alex, as second-in-command, moved to the front in order to address the others.

'We've done it a couple of times but never with both squadrons involved,' one of the sergeant pilots said. The speaker looked no more than eighteen or nineteen – too young to have so much responsibility. 'We've never gone up in more than pairs at night.'

'I've got less experience than anyone here. However, I can see a major flaw in this plan. Even with instruments, radar and instructions over the RT, it's going to be bloody difficult picking friend from foe. I'm going to speak to the CO. Hang about here, I won't be long. Get the map down, Tommy, and see exactly where we're supposed to be going.'

He found Wing Commander Sugden in his office. 'Take a pew, old bean. No need for you to tell me why you're here. Bloody stupid for an entire squadron to go up at once, but that's what we've got to do.'

'Any suggestions, sir?'

'You're in charge in the air, old boy. What do you intend to do?'

'I thought if we fly in pairs, keep a safe distance between us, we're less likely to fire on each other. I assume Fighter Command will be plotting and will give us sufficient warning of any bandits in the vicinity.'

'The 109s, the elite of the Luftwaffe, are thin on the ground. This is a final push by Hitler. God knows why he's not concentrating his efforts on defence. Attacking England is pointless in his position.'

'The man's barking, and Goering's no better. I would have thought the powers that be would be better keeping us for the invasion. We've got plenty of fighters but not many Rocket Typhoons.'

'I said exactly the same. However, I'm reliably informed that this is likely to be the last major incursion we're asked to perform before D-Day. It's all very hush-hush, of course, but preparations are well in hand and we should be heading for France in a couple of months.'

This was the news that Alex had been expecting but dreading. 'From that, I take it we're likely to be based in France rather than here?'

'Depends how quickly the army can prepare a safe place for us to fly from. Should have asked; how's the wife and baby?'

'Julia, my daughter, was never in any danger. Thank God my wife's now making a full recovery. Thank you for asking.'

He returned to the ops room and gave the men the gen. He didn't tell them everything he'd learnt. 'My squadron will depart first. Get something to eat and a few hours' kip. Those of us in the first show will be called at midnight. Everyone here is familiar with the territory and the kind of operation involved although it's going to be a lot trickier in the dark.'

He grabbed something to eat and then retreated to his room. He should have stretched out on his bed and got some sleep right away but instead he wrote to Babs.

Darling,

I hated to leave you in hospital but had no choice. Things will be different once you're home and hopefully you'll be able to put aside your sadness and just be thankful we have a perfect family.

I doubt that I'll get any leave in the foreseeable but if I get a moment I'll ring. I love you and never doubt for one second that I don't consider Charlie as much my son as Julia is my daughter.

We both wanted more children but we're lucky to have the two we've got. When you feel better, write to me. I love getting your letters. When you're home ask Tom to take a snap of the three of you so I can put it in my wallet.

This past week has been traumatic but we've come through it.

All my love,

Alex

He quickly added the address of the hospital and licked the stamp. His orderly would see it went into the postbag tomorrow. He'd had to write another letter to be given to Babs if he went for a Burton. He'd been reluctant to do so as last time the letter had been sent when he was still alive.

This bloody war had gone on for years and somehow, despite the odds against it, he was still alive. He just had to get through the next few months and then, with luck, it would be over and he could return to The Grove and take care of his family.

If it didn't end soon then his brother Jim, and Tom – Babs's brother – would be expected to enlist. That didn't bear thinking of. Joe, Mrs B's only child, was already in the army and that was quite bad enough.

* * *

Almost three weeks after her dramatic departure from her home Babs returned, this time with a baby in her arms. Grandpa had managed to borrow a car to collect them – heaven knows where he'd got the petrol for it – and they travelled home in style.

Julia was thriving, putting on weight and already holding up her head and taking an interest in the world about her. As Barbara's wound had healed and she'd been able to feed her daughter without discomfort, the bond between them had begun to form.

Charlie had only come in once to the hospital right at the start. He'd been subdued, not his usual self, and after taking one look at the baby had then ignored her. Babs feared there were going to be problems. Her son had been the centre of attention, adored by six adults, and now he would have to share this with his sister.

Although, for Alex's sake, she was pleased that Julia had red hair she wished her daughter looked like her. Girls were supposed to take after their mother not their father. Having one red-headed child and one with blond hair was bound to draw comment eventually – if not from Charlie then from her brothers.

Why wasn't she happy? She'd come to terms with the loss of her womb, that her husband was once more in permanent danger. She really didn't know why she was finding it so hard to enjoy the new baby.

Grandpa had said not being able to breastfeed would make bonding slower, that things would improve once she was at home surrounded by her family.

The car drove around the side of the house and pulled up outside the back door. Grandpa turned off the engine and swivelled round to look at her on the back seat with the baby.

'Things will get better, my dear girl. You're a bit down at the moment and that's only to be expected. Let your relationship with Julia develop naturally – don't try and force things. Are you ready to go in?'

She blinked back unwanted tears. 'Not really. I'm a different person now whilst the rest of you are still the same. I just want to give the baby to someone else and pretend this never happened.'

'I know you do, but that wouldn't help anyone and would just make things worse. Your grandma and I will do everything necessary to help you over this tricky patch. Charlie's been cutting out paper bunting and helping Mrs B prepare a welcome-home party for both of you.'

The last thing she wanted was a fuss. 'I'm not well enough for anything like that. I'm going straight to bed.' She paused and said what she'd been thinking for the past few days. 'I'm going to employ a nanny to take care of the baby. That will be better for her and for me.'

She waited until he opened the car door and then handed the

baby over to him. Her tummy was still uncomfortable and clambering out would be impossible whilst holding her. She hurried inside, didn't take Julia back, and dashed straight up the stairs without going into the kitchen where she could hear voices.

Once in the safety of her bedroom she closed the door and turned the key in the lock. Everything necessary for the care of the infant had been, on her instructions, moved into the nursery – a small bedroom adjacent to Charlie's. If she stayed where she was someone else could take care of both of them and she could get some much-needed sleep.

It had been impossible to sleep properly in hospital as it was far too noisy. In a few days she would feel well enough to get up and interact with her son and the rest of the family. Now all she wanted was privacy, silence and sleep.

She locked herself in the bathroom and filled the tub with double the amount of water she was supposed to use. A long, hot soak was exactly what she needed. Also, in here she couldn't hear if anyone banged on her bedroom door.

When Alex had discovered that Charlie was John's son, he had kicked in the lock on the bathroom door. There was no one here who would do anything like that. She was safe. The livid scar that ran from her navel all the way down had healed well but would be a constant reminder that she was no longer a real woman. If Alex left her for someone who could give him the son he didn't have then she wouldn't blame him.

She remained where she was until the water was tepid, her skin wrinkled, and she was shivering. She hadn't used this enormous bath for several months as getting out was difficult at the best of times. Despite the fact that she was no longer heavily pregnant she still had to roll over onto her knees and then cling on to the sides in order to stand up.

She dried herself hurriedly, unlocked the door and went in

search of a warm nightgown. Then she tumbled into bed and pulled the blankets over her head. It took a while for her to warm up and feel comfortable.

There was no one outside in the passageway. They must've come and then, because she'd been so long in the bath, had gone away. Her stomach rumbled loudly. She glanced at the carriage clock ticking noisily on the mantelpiece. Only five o'clock – it would be hours before the house was quiet and she could creep down and find herself something to eat.

Although she was desperate for the oblivion of sleep she remained restless and wide awake. Why hadn't she heard the baby crying, Charlie asking for her? Tom and David hadn't knocked on the door and pleaded with her to come out.

She got up and pulled on her dressing gown. It was as if there was an unseen weight pressing down on her, making everything she did a huge effort of will. She sat on the edge of the bed and tried to pull herself together. Charlie must be devastated that his mummy hadn't bothered to come and say hello. However miserable she was, it wasn't his fault.

Walking to the door and unlocking it was a small step. She opened it but somehow couldn't make her feet walk through. If she called out would someone hear her? She couldn't find the energy to do so. The fire was dying down, there was a full scuttle of coal as well as logs waiting to be put on, but just the thought of doing something so energetic defeated her.

She flopped into the armchair and closed her eyes. If Alex were here things would be different.

5

Alex and his squadron returned relatively unscathed from their night-time manoeuvres. They had two definites and one probable hit but it was hard to tell in the dark. The second wave of Rocket Typhoons had left half an hour after them so debrief wouldn't be until they were all back.

He congratulated his men, commiserated with the two that had bullet holes in their kites but not in themselves, and they heaved themselves into the waiting lorry. God – was it only six o'clock? He didn't envy the poor buggers who flew every night to bomb an unfortunate German city. The Yanks had proved useless at night flying so now their bombers did the daytime runs, leaving the more dangerous work to the RAF.

The intelligence bods asked their usual questions, logbooks were filled in and then after scoffing down a large breakfast they headed for their billets. The other two squadrons were now on readiness, but hopefully they wouldn't be scrambled today. The Rocket Typhoons were the best ground-to-air attack fighters the RAF had at their disposal. This wing was going to be crucial in the invasion.

* * *

The next two weeks were spent perfecting their low-flying skills with occasional forays across the channel for the intelligence bods. Knowing what the Germans were doing in preparation for the imminent arrival of the Allied forces was vital.

Exactly when and where this would take place was a secret even from those who would be at the forefront of the attack – themselves. After a week the squadrons exchanged rotas, which meant he would be back on nights again from tomorrow.

This gave him a few hours to himself. Drinking was frowned upon during the day so no alcohol was served in the officers' mess until later. This didn't stop the determined chaps who would pedal down to the village and grab a pint or two at the local hostelry. He wasn't one of them.

Babs would have had one night at home now and hopefully be back to her old self. He'd had regular reports from Edward on her progress in hospital and had also spoken to Charlie. His son was missing his mother desperately and the longer she was away the more the little chap began to resent his new sister.

As a senior officer he had access to a telephone in an office and didn't have to queue to use the public telephone outside the ops room. Elspeth answered – he'd hoped it would be Babs.

'How is Babs? She must be so pleased to be home. Can I speak to her?'

'I'm afraid that you can't, Alex. Things are not going at all well. She is refusing to have anything to do with Julia and locked herself in your bedroom last night.'

'What the hell for? Charlie told me he was planning a welcome-home party – are you telling me that she didn't bother to go? That's not like her at all.'

'It certainly isn't. Edward said that it's something to do with postnatal depression. Having such a traumatic birth, it appears, can do this to a new mother. Charlie won't go and see her and is being a real handful at the moment. We're just too old to deal with all this fuss.'

He bit back a terse retort. Why was she telling him this when there was nothing he could do about it? There was a bloody war on – surely to God there were enough of them there to take care of Babs and the two little ones?

Elspeth continued before he'd framed a suitable response. 'She says she's going to get a nanny and doesn't want to look after the baby herself.'

'In which case that solves the problem, doesn't it? I'd like to speak to my son, please.'

'The boys have taken him and the dogs out. Edward said fresh air and exercise will do them all good. I'll give Babs your love. Do you know when you might get any leave again?'

'I won't get any leave for the next few months. We're about to invade France and finish this damn war. Some families haven't seen the man of the house for years. I'm sure Babs and the children can manage without me until it's over. Tell her I love her and am writing to her today. Give Charlie my love as well.'

He put the receiver down more forcefully than he'd intended. First John had cracked up and now his beloved girl was struggling. He dialled one hundred and asked the operator to connect him to his parents' farm.

After he'd explained how worried he was about Babs and Charlie, his mother reassured him. 'I'm not surprised she's in a bit of a state, Alex. I'll cycle over and see her tomorrow. I can't wait to meet my new grandchild. I wonder if Valerie's new baby will have red hair like your daughter.'

Alex felt better after talking to Mum. When his sister Valerie's baby had died suddenly when she was just nine months old, his sister had fallen into a deep depression. In fact, it hadn't been until she'd had another child that she was back to being anywhere near her old self.

Babs and Valerie had been good friends until that point but his sister had found it too hard remaining in contact when Babs had Charlie and she had nothing. He would be abusing his privilege by using the phone a third time but he thought it would be worth giving his sister a ring and asking her if she would visit if she could.

Then he reconsidered. There was no petrol available for civilians and even farms were running short. What they had was meant for tractors and not social jaunts around the countryside. Every gallon was going to be needed when the big push came.

Thousands of the brown jobs had been footling around in army camps since Dunkirk. They'd had no battle experience and it was going to be hard for them being pitched head first into France in a couple of months and being expected to defeat what was left of the experienced German army.

Unlike the desert rats who had been fighting in Africa for years – he couldn't imagine anything worse than being stranded in the desert with nothing but sand and not a tree in sight. There were squadrons based all over the world and he was fortunate to have spent the majority of the war based in Hornchurch.

Babs was strong – she'd get through this. Hadn't she survived a lifetime of abuse from her lunatic mother? When he'd been declared missing, presumed dead she'd carried on, not given in to grief, and he had every confidence in a few weeks she would be back to her usual jolly self.

***

Every day was a struggle. Babs dragged herself out of bed feeling ancient. Grandpa had explained it wasn't her fault, that feeling depressed after a difficult delivery was quite common. She had to make an effort for her children's sake.

Elspeth had said taking care of Julia was too much for her, and Mrs B was far too busy running the house to do more than keep an eye on Charlie occasionally. Her brothers were out all day at school and even when they were home, they had so much homework it wouldn't be fair to ask them to help her.

She'd placed an advert in *The Lady* for a live-in nanny but so far had had no response. This wasn't surprising as every woman not looking after her own children now had to enlist for war work of some sort.

'Mummy, that baby's crying again. It's making my head hurt.' Charlie scowled and stamped his foot.

'I expect she needs a bottle. Julia's a good baby and only cries when she wants something.' She scooped up her daughter and rested the screaming bundle against her shoulder. 'Come along, sweetheart, we've got to go downstairs now. Would you like to help me feed her this time?'

'I wouldn't. I don't like smelly babies. Why didn't you bring me back a boy?'

'Daddy and I didn't have any choice – but we're both delighted to have a son and a daughter. You've already got Tom and David who play with you all the time.'

'I'm not coming with you to the kitchen. I'm going upstairs to play with the train set. Buttons and Patch are coming with me.'

Julia was at full throttle, screaming for her feed. 'I don't have time to argue with you. Your little sister is hungry and you're a big boy and should know better.'

Mrs B had heard the racket and the milk was already warm and waiting in the kitchen. 'Thank you – you're a lifesaver.' Babs snatched up the glass bottle and pushed the rubber teat into Julia's mouth.

'Fine pair of lungs on that baby, Mrs Everton. I shouldn't worry about your little boy not taking to her. Once she's smiling at him, he'll soon come around.'

'I hope you're right. I'm going to take Julia upstairs again – I don't like to leave Charlie on his own at the moment.'

The baby continued to suck noisily, unbothered by being carried around the place. She trudged up to the nursery floor and sat in the comfortable armchair in front of the fire where she could watch her son playing.

Julia was five weeks old today. Although she wanted spring to be over, everyone knew that as soon as the weather improved the invasion would start. Alex was due to telephone this afternoon. He only managed to call her when he was on nights.

Charlie had stopped fiddling with his train set and was moving towards her. She deliberately ignored his approach. Julia was on her shoulder while she rubbed her back to bring up her wind. Just as her son arrived at her knee the baby belched loudly and then broke wind.

'I didn't know she could do that. Did I make rude noises when I was a baby?' Charlie was laughing, looking at his sister with more interest than he'd shown so far.

'You certainly did. I've got to give her the other half of her bottle. She can't drink it all at once or she gets tummy ache.'

He was leaning against her knee and didn't shy away when Julia's head was touching him. She held her breath as he reached out and touched the flaming red hair.

'I like her hair now – it's just like daddy's. I've got hair like Tom and David. Nobody's got hair like you – a brown colour.'

'Grandpa used to have the same colour hair as me. He's still got the curls.'

'Why is his hair grey now?'

'Hair goes grey as people get older. I expect mine will go grey one day.'

Julia stop sucking and spat out the teat. She was staring at Charlie and then she smiled. It could be wind but Babs thought it was her daughter's very first smile.

Charlie moved closer. 'She smiled at me, Mummy. Does she like me?'

'Of course she does – you're her big brother. I don't think she wants any more milk, do you? She's far too interested in you.'

'If you bang her back again will she make more rude noises?'

'Shall we see?'

Julia obliged and this time the rude noises were accompanied by a smell. Charlie wrinkled his nose and laughed. 'I think she's done a poo-poo, Mummy. Are you going to change her nappy?'

'I certainly am. Could you please bring me the blanket from the top of that chest of drawers and put it down on the mat?' He ran over willingly and brought back the blanket. Babs gently put the baby on the floor.

Charlie watched closely. 'She hasn't got a tinkle like me. Is that why she's a girl baby?'

'It is. Now, I've just got to put on her rubber pants and then she's done. She'll sleep now until she's hungry again.'

He lost interest and wandered back to his train set. There was a spare bassinet in the nursery so she didn't have to keep running up and down stairs. Julia was no trouble at all. She kissed her downy head and put her down.

She gazed down at the sleeping infant, so like her daddy, and unexpectedly a wave of love engulfed her. Her knees almost gave way. The blackness that had been pressing her down didn't seem as heavy. She wasn't fully recovered but truly believed the worst was over.

'Mummy, can you help me wind up the engine? It's very tricky for me.'

The two of them were still happily playing trains when Grandpa came in, followed by Grandma carrying a very welcome tray of tea and biscuits. There was a clatter on the stairs and Tom came in.

'Don't worry, big sis, we've got the afternoon free. The boiler packed up and everyone's been sent home,' Tom said. 'Dave's bringing up another tray. Mrs B has just made scones.'

'It seems such a long time since we've all been together. If only Joe and Alex were here it would be perfect,' she said as she smiled up at her two enormous, grown-up brothers.

'Mrs B is keeping a brave face about it, Babs, but I reckon she's worried sick. Joe was lucky not to have been posted abroad but—'

'Not a good idea to talk about such things, Tom,' Grandpa cut in, 'in front of you know who. Let's keep conversations about the war until the evening.'

'Sorry, Grandad. I keep forgetting that he might be only three but understands and talks like a much older child,' Tom said as he munched through his third scone.

Charlie had scrambled onto her lap, not something he'd done since she'd come back from hospital because her tummy had been too sore. She loved the feel of him pressed against her and she pushed back his floppy blond hair. She'd hidden her photo of John, as her son's likeness to his biological father was quite startling.

'I'm three, Mummy. I'm a big boy now.'

'You are, darling, and now you're a big brother as well as a big boy.'

He sighed, settled back, put his thumb in his mouth and fell asleep. 'I think he's accepted the new arrival, don't you, Grandpa?'

'I do, my dear girl, and you seem a lot better too. All we want is for this bloody war to be over and things will be perfect.'

'Edward, moderate your language, please.'

Grandpa chuckled. 'That was moderate, Elspeth. Any more tea in the pot, David, for a thirsty old man?'

The impromptu party broke up when Mrs B called up the nursery stairs that Alex was on the phone. Tom jumped to his feet and carefully lifted Charlie from her lap. She smiled her thanks and rushed off to take the call.

'Alex, darling, I'm so glad to speak to you.'

'And I to you, sweetheart. You sound more cheerful. Are you feeling a bit better?'

She happily explained what had happened and she could almost feel his relief coming over the line.

'I've been so worried about you, darling. Now I can concentrate on staying alive and coming back to you all when this lot is over. There's someone from HQ here to talk to us, so I have to go. Kiss the children for me. Love you.'

'I love you too. Keep safe, Alex.' He didn't answer. The line was dead.

For the first time in weeks she was able to be more optimistic about their future. She was coming out of her black moods, Charlie was more comfortable with the idea of having a sister, and she had finally bonded with her gorgeous little daughter.

* * *

May was drawing to a close and The Grove was now a harmonious household. Babs was revelling in being the mother of two wonderful children and was able to help Mrs B as well as take care of Charlie and Julia.

One evening after supper, the children were asleep. They all, apart from David who was catching up with some schoolwork, gathered in the sitting room to listen to *ITMA*, the most popular programme on the wireless, and then the nine o'clock news. Tom announced that he had a girlfriend, Pricilla, a young lady from the Ursuline, a convent school for girls also in Brentwood. He jokingly told them that it was wearing the obligatory sixth form boater and carrying a prefect's cane that had won her over.

'I hope it's not going to interfere with your studies, young man,' Grandpa said.

'Absolutely not. We just meet for a walk and an orange squash in the café. Her parents would have a fit if it was anything more. I'd like to invite her to tea; would that be all right?'

Grandpa nodded. 'Of course it would. We'd love to meet any friends of yours. When were you thinking?'

'What about tomorrow? I'll ask her now and she can tell her olds that she's going to be late home.'

'Why doesn't she stay the night? I'll speak to her parents if you like?' Grandma offered.

'Would you? That would be spiffing. Will be easier for her to get home on a Saturday. She lives in Brentwood. Her father's a solicitor and her mother's very posh.'

Grandpa laughed. 'Then she will fit right in.'

Her brother rushed off to make the call accompanied by Grandma. 'How can he be old enough to have a girlfriend, Grandpa?'

'Shocking, isn't it? Before you know it, Charlie will be at school and Julia will be running about.' He frowned. 'Tom and Jim will be called up soon enough if this bloody war isn't over.'

'Don't even say that. It's hard enough having Alex still involved; the thought of my little brother fighting is unbearable.'

'Even if the Germans are defeated there'll still be conscription. It might be a year or two after the actual end of hostilities before things get back to normal.'

'Both Tom and Jim are officer cadets and I know they want to serve and will be off like a shot if asked.'

'I think they can have conscription deferred if they're going to university. Nothing to worry about, my dear.'

'When Joe came back last month I felt he behaved as if it was his last visit. Didn't you think so?'

'You were imagining it, my dear. Good, Elspeth and Tom are here just in time as *ITMA* is about to start.'

'I'm going to give it a miss, Grandpa. I don't like leaving Julia alone upstairs when the radio's on.' She kissed him on his leathery cheek and dashed off, calling a cheerful goodnight to the others as she left.

6

Babs wasn't sure how many of the family should be present when Priscilla arrived with Tom. It might be a bit overwhelming for her to have everyone milling about. She decided to take Julia – in the old-fashioned, coach-built pram – and Charlie to visit her in-laws at Home Farm.

'It's lovely to see you, Babs. You've arrived just in time for a nice cuppa,' Mrs Everton said as she scooped up Charlie and gave him a sloppy kiss. He wriggled to get down and ran in ahead of them.

'Julia will need a feed whilst we're here. I've got her bottle made up so just need to put it in a jug of warm water.'

'Such a shame you couldn't feed her yourself, so much more convenient.' Her mother-in-law stared fondly at her newest grandchild. 'It's strange how Alex, Valerie and Jim have red hair like my hubby, but only Ned has mouse-brown hair like mine.'

'But Valerie's second daughter didn't inherit her colouring. I wonder if her next baby will be more like Julia.'

'I've been wondering about that too. It's a miracle there's another baby coming soon as Pete only gets leave from the base occasionally. In fact, what with the invasion coming any day, he's not been home at all for weeks. Alex rang this morning and said you were feeling better. You certainly look more like the Babs you used to be.'

Babs patted her still far too rounded stomach. 'I've still got quite a lot of weight to lose before I'm back to my old shape. I took Silver out for a hack this morning for the first time in months. I really missed being able to ride.'

She left the pram with the sleeping infant outside the kitchen window so they could keep an eye on her. Patch and Buttons had flopped down beside her daughter, which meant that none of the yard cats would come anywhere near.

The two farm collies must be out with her father-in-law as they hadn't come to greet her when she arrived. They were good friends with her dogs so even if they did come back there'd not be any fuss.

Charlie was so familiar with this house that he immediately went to the cupboard in the larder to find himself a jigsaw to do at the large, scrubbed pine table that dominated the centre of the kitchen.

'Nanna, Julia smiled at me first. I'm her very favourite person,' he announced.

'I'm not surprised to hear that, Charlie. You're my favourite grandson. Now, do you want your milk hot or cold?'

'No milk, I don't like it any more. I like water best, Nanna.'

'Well, I've got plenty of that. Climb up on your chair and I'll fetch you a nice piece of cake to go with your water.'

Whilst her son was engrossed with the puzzle Babs had time to talk without interruption. 'Tom's bringing over a girlfriend for tea. Has Jim found himself a young lady too?'

'Not that he's mentioned. Mind you, the two of them are thick as thieves. If your Tom is taking an interest in the girls then I'm quite sure my Jim will be doing the same. They both look so grown-up – I've had some ladies commenting at the WI that Jim should be in uniform. I thank God that I've only got Alex to worry about.'

'Grandpa thinks they'll still have to serve even if the war's over but not if they go to university. Both my brothers are determined to be doctors. What about your two? Has Jim made up his mind yet what he wants to do when he leaves school in a couple of years?'

'The only thing he's certain about is that he doesn't want to farm so it's a good thing that Ned is going to follow in his father's footsteps. I think Jim might go to Sandhurst if he can get in. He seems to enjoy being an officer cadet at school.'

'A career soldier? I'm surprised he doesn't want to join the RAF like his brother did. Alex is a regular, but I hope he's not signing on again. He's only got one more year and then he'll be free to leave if the war's over.'

'I know he intends to take over your grandfather's business interests, run the estate and so on. But I thought you might like to have a house of your own – you can certainly afford it.'

'Alex promised Grandpa he would take care of things until Tom and David are old enough to do so. Grandpa's leaving The Grove and everything else to them. I've got more than enough in my trust fund.' Talking about a time when her beloved grandfather was no longer with them was upsetting and she quickly changed the subject.

'My grandmother has been pestering me to arrange for Julia to be baptised but I don't want to do it until Alex can be there. What does Valerie intend to do about her new baby when it comes?'

'She said exactly the same as you. Why don't we have a joint baptism next year when everyone can be here? I know it's unusual to wait until the baby's a toddler but the fathers need to be there too.'

After feeding and changing Julia it was time to begin the two-mile walk home. Charlie sat in the end of the pram with his feet dangling over and spent the entire time reciting his latest nursery rhyme – she was heartily sick of Humpty Dumpty and hoped he'd soon move on to something different.

She left the pram in the study where she could hear if Julia cried and then took Charlie's hand and they walked into the sitting room to meet Tom's friend.

Priscilla was a tall girl with ash-blonde hair, bright blue eyes and a lovely warm smile. 'Mrs Everton, I'm so glad to meet you.' She held out her hand and Babs shook it enthusiastically.

'Please, Priscilla, call me Babs. This is Charlie.'

Her son had been hiding behind her knees but peeped out and smiled. 'P'cilla's a funny name. I like it.'

'I'd have known you anywhere, Charlie. You look just like your uncles. Is your sister asleep?'

'She did a big poo but she's clean now.'

'That's quite enough talking about that sort of thing, young man. You need to wash your hands and face before you join us for tea,' Grandma said firmly.

'As do I. Excuse us for a moment whilst we make ourselves presentable.'

* * *

After supper Babs joined in a noisy and highly competitive game of Monopoly with her brothers and Priscilla. Her grandparents had retired early. Each player took it in turns to listen at the bottom of the stairs for the children, but neither Charlie nor Julia made a sound.

'I'm just going to prepare the ten o'clock feed for my daughter. I've been soundly trounced but have had such a good time. I do hope you'll come again, Priscilla, and maybe next time we can form a coalition and beat the boys.'

'I'd love to. I promised Ma that I'd catch the first bus. Unfortunately, it leaves at half past seven so I doubt I'll see you in the morning. Thank you so much for making me welcome.'

'Then, goodbye and I hope to see you again very soon.'

It didn't occur to her until she was comfortable and dropping off to sleep that Tom and Priscilla could easily spend the night together if that's what they wanted to do as nobody would be any the wiser. Her brother was certainly a young adult, quite capable of making love to his girlfriend, but he was also a gentleman and wouldn't dream of doing so – and they were both under age.

* * *

By the end of May every road was filled with army lorries. No one was allowed off the base. The entire wing was on readiness for the imminent invasion. On the evening of 5th of June Alex and his second in command, newly promoted Flying Officer Billy Jarvis, were summoned to intelligence.

'Right, you two bods,' the intelligence chappie said, 'you've got to fly south of Brest. Keep well away from the coastline of the Cherbourg Peninsula, and report on cloud conditions in that area.' He gestured to the map and they followed his finger carefully.

'Maintain RT silence and in no circumstances engage enemy aircraft or fire on anything at sea. Is that clear?'

'Absolutely crystal,' Alex replied. He'd done several of these weather recces and could see nothing out of the ordinary about this one.

'Bloody horrible weather for the past few days, Alex, but excellent today. It will be a piece of cake, don't you think?' Billy said as they headed for the truck to take them to their kites.

'I do. Nothing we haven't done before. Did you notice those

brown jobs, high-ranking officers, hanging about? Something's up – I think it's all about to kick off.'

He and Billy left Holmsley South and climbed steadily on the designated course in perfect evening sunshine. When the squadron went out they always flew at wave-top level to avoid German radar, but not today. Although they flew in tandem, because they had to maintain radio silence it was the same as flying alone.

Nothing of any importance happened. The Cherbourg Peninsula was quiet and, as far as he could see, the Atlantic was empty. Nothing but high cirrus clouds indicating the approach of frontal systems. This was all he'd have to report when he returned.

He'd seen no sign of any Luftwaffe kites or heard any German gunners in the port open fire on them. As he approached the south coast he was astonished to see that from Poole, right across to Portsmouth and beyond, the sea was packed with ships crawling out of estuaries and inlets.

He peered out of his cockpit knowing he was seeing history in the making. He was witnessing the D-Day armada gathering. Ships of all descriptions containing thousands of soldiers and their equipment were slowly heading for the Normandy coast.

Operation Overlord was no longer a secret as far as he was concerned. When he'd left France the coast had been quiet, but so had the English beach; now everything had changed. How was it possible an invasion was underway and yet the Germans seemed unaware of it?

He landed first and taxied from the apron; Billy came down minutes later. The importance and secrecy of what they'd seen in the Channel was brought home to them when armed guards surrounded them as they clambered from the aircraft.

The intelligence bod heard their report on the weather in silence. 'D-Day is underway, chaps, but you'll understand that we have to keep you under armed guard until things have moved forward.'

'I don't understand at all. Do you think we're suddenly a security risk? Bloody stupid, if you ask me,' Alex said.

'Nobody is asking you, Squadron Leader Everton. You will be held under armed guard whether you like it or not until we deem it safe for you to be released.'

Several hours later, around midnight, the guards escorted them back to intelligence. This time the room was packed with every pilot from the wing as well as a large sprinkling of officers from other services. The room was thick with tobacco smoke and the atmosphere was tense.

'Where the hell have you two been? Thought you'd gone for a Burton,' one of his flight asked.

Alex had no time to answer as the wing co and other top brass marched in. There was no need for him to ask for quiet.

'Operation Overlord is now underway, gentlemen. I have to inform you that British, Canadian and American paratroopers are dropping into Normandy to capture vital targets.'

It took a few seconds for the words to sink in and then the room erupted in cheers and catcalls. The blokes were on their feet, slapping each other on the back and shaking hands. This moment had been a long time coming and he was as excited as everyone else.

The invasion had finally begun – it was the beginning of the end of this gruelling nightmare of a war. The noise abated when the brown job undid the strings holding the cover over a large map. The canvas dropped away. Hanging there was a massive map of the Normandy coast from the Ouistreham estuary to the base of the Cherbourg Peninsula in the west. With great precision the officer carefully outlined what was going to happen and exactly what the Allied forces were going to be doing.

Alex noticed that many of the pilots were yawning, looking

bored, only interested in what exactly their own role would be. He wasn't one of them – he didn't understand their attitude. Surely, many of them must have relatives who were heading for France and possible death?

The army chap finished his brief and the wing co took his place. Now everyone was alert and listening carefully to the gen.

'You chaps in your Rocket Typhoons will be patrolling behind the area of the beaches. Your job is to shoot up German reinforcements being brought in to neutralise the Allied landings. Gun positions: Panzer and SS Headquarters are priority targets. However, anything spotted on the roads is fair game.

'Spitfires will take care of anything flying above you and that will allow you to operate without having to worry about Luftwaffe fighters.'

Alex raised his hand and Sugden nodded. 'Are we still flying low, sir?'

'Good question, Everton. No need for subterfuge any more. I was going on to explain how things are going to work. Clever devils, these D-Day planners. They've divided the air into corridors to avoid collisions. Lower layers for ground-attack fighters, we fly between 1500 and 3500 feet. Next medium and heavy bombers, and the upper layer for fighter cover.

'Any other questions? Good – take-off at 04.45. Navigation lights on – flying at 3000 feet. We're to make an armed recce south of Caen.'

After the briefing the men wandered back to their billets or their appropriate messes, laughing and celebrating as if they'd been given the best possible news. He was one of the older pilots, had more battle experience than any of them, and he couldn't see what was coming as something to celebrate.

There was no question that the Allied forces were going to win, but at what cost? How many of these young men would die over the next few weeks? More to the point how many thousands of soldiers would be lost in the ensuing battles?

His squadron and one other were in the first wave to leave. It was going to be strange taking off with navigation lights on. When they jumped out of the trucks, instead of the usual silence there was a buzz of conversation, the flashing of shaded torches and vehicle lights.

He spoke some reassuring words to the young men who were less experienced at night flying than he was. 'It's going to be tricky fumbling around in the cockpit with only the dim light from your instruments to see by. Keep calm, just think of this as another routine flight that simply happens to be at night. Make sure you plug in your leads, adjust your oxygen, clip on your parachute and harness correctly and do your cockpit check before starting up.'

There was a murmur of agreement from the men and then they dispersed to their own kites and began to scramble in. The Sabre engine's throaty roar was quite audible in the cockpit. He was leading from the front and the flyer he was paired with would have to follow his navigation lights.

Thirty-two Typhoons thundered down the runway and began to climb into the night sky. Four squadrons in total were now on their way to Normandy. Each squadron's kites were stacked in twos, one under the other in two flights of four.

He sent up a quick prayer that all the boys would return safely and then concentrated on doing what he was trained for: leading his men in a fighter-bomber attack against the enemy.

The RT barked out the order to switch off nav lights. He looked down and could just make out the dim outline of hundreds of ships heading for the Normandy coast. Battleships, cruisers and destroyers were positioned in a huge semicircle firing continuously at the Germans as the naval battle began.

As they crossed the coastline there was the occasional burst of black smoke as the German flak batteries began to fire. The red and yellow tracer bullets arced through the sky but as far as he could see no one in the wing had been hit.

Moments later the Typhoons were through the flak and, as the wing leader, he gave the command to attack. 'Line astern, go!' Immediately all thirty-two kites split from their formations and tucked in one behind the other in a single line and headed for the enemy below.

There was now heavy cloud building up and the landscape was obscured by it as he led the dive towards Caen. The town was already smoking from the bombs dropped earlier. The Typhoons burst through a hole in the cloud like a terrifying conga line and he pulled out of a steep dive at 1000 feet.

The RT crackled and demanded that they split up and go in search of prey. The line broke up and went in search of any movement of German troops on the main roads, but they were empty. Alex had expected to see columns of Germans heading into the Caen area. How could such a massive operation not be noticed by their enemy?

He flew low along the road. Yes – there was a flash of something silver hiding in the woods. He and his partner dived down to take a closer look and the Germans opened fire. The remainder of the wing were circling below the clouds and an easy target for the gunners. He gave the order for them to go in with their rockets.

He sprayed the trees with cannon shells, hoping to keep the gunners hiding. One Typhoon exploded and he saw several others hit by flak. They wouldn't all be returning tonight. He just hoped the sacrifice of his men had been worth it and the Germans' hidden gun emplacement was totally destroyed.

7

The Grove was a place of mourning. Three days after D-Day began, Mrs B had received the dreaded telegram saying that Joe had died within a few hours of landing in Normandy. Babs didn't expect Alex to ring her and was sick with fear that she would be the next one to receive bad news.

As it was the half-term break, Jim Everton had been staying when the news arrived. David had gone to stay with Ned. The boys took it particularly badly. Initially they were silent, eyes tear-filled, unable to do more than hug Mrs B to show their sympathy. Then the two of them retreated upstairs.

When they didn't come down for the hastily put together supper that she'd prepared Babs went in search of them. The room they shared was empty.

'Grandpa, Tom and Jim aren't here. I'm going to ring and see if they've gone to Home Farm to tell Ned and David in person.'

'Poor Mrs B. She's lost not just a son, but her only living relative. Elspeth's with her, but she's inconsolable.'

'It brings back that dreadful time when Marigold was

murdered. There must be hundreds of families in pieces this morning.'

'Make your telephone call, my dear, and then we must talk.'

When the operator connected her Mrs Everton answered.

'Have Tom and Jim come over to you?'

'No, they aren't here. Is there something wrong, Babs? You sound really upset.'

She gave her the bad news about Joe. 'I haven't seen my brother or Jim since this morning. Where on earth could they have gone? It must be something to do with Joe's death – but I can't think what it might be.'

'I'll tell Ned and David. Let me know when you find them. Don't worry, they're young men now and can look after themselves.'

The cold supper was ignored. Grandpa came in and she replaced the receiver on the handset. 'It won't be dark for a few hours yet, my dear. No need to worry until then. I think it likely they've gone into Brentwood to be with their friends.'

'I expect you're right. What did you want to talk about, Grandpa?'

'Mrs B will be in no fit state to run the house for a while. There aren't any women available to help from the village so we've got to manage ourselves.' He paused and his expression worried her. 'I'm sure you've noticed that Elspeth isn't quite herself any more. She's forgetting things, gets easily confused. I fear that she is showing signs of senile dementia.'

'I've been so busy with my own problems that I really hadn't noticed. Grandma is still as loving and kind as she's always been. But now you come to mention it, I did think it odd that she'd stopped going to the WI and the WVS. What can I do to help?'

'I'm hoping that you can take over the cooking as well as looking after the little ones. Are you up to that?'

'I'm much better now. My brothers can help with the housework as well as doing the outside jobs. We'll muddle through.'

'Excellent. I'll look after Elspeth and Mrs B. Why don't you have a look in Tom's bedroom? There might be some clue as to where they've gone in there.'

'Good idea, Grandpa. It's not like either of them to rush off without telling someone. It has to be to do with Joe's death. I can't believe that lovely young man has gone. I remember when I first met him all those years ago, he said he was glad that Mrs B was going to live with us as if anything happened to him in the war she'd have us to take care of her.'

She wiped her eyes and sniffed. 'I never thought this beastly war would go on so long and that he would actually have to fight.'

Grandpa patted her on the shoulder and she rushed upstairs, swallowing the lump in her throat. Her brothers had chosen to remain on the top floor where the playroom was, even though they could have moved down and been with everyone else on the first floor.

She'd looked in here ages ago and wasn't sure what she was expecting to find. She stood in the doorway staring and realised something that should be here was missing. Jim's overnight bag wasn't there. She looked in the walk-in closet and discovered Tom's was also missing.

They were intending to be away overnight – but where would they have gone? She checked in the nursery and in Charlie's room before racing downstairs again. Could they have gone to Priscilla's house? She thought it unlikely but decided to make the call anyway.

When Tom's girlfriend came to the phone Babs quickly explained why she was ringing. 'Have you any idea where the two of them might have gone?'

'I'm sorry, I don't. They were both very fond of Joe and often spoke of him. I'm so sorry for your loss, Mrs Everton. If Tom contacts me then I'll let you know at once. I think he's probably gone to Town to drown his sorrows with Jim.'

'I sincerely hope you're right. Goodnight, Priscilla.'

Tom and Jim were still youngsters but looked much older. They could hardly go to the local pub where they were known if they wanted to get drunk, so going to London sounded like the answer. Tom got a regular allowance and would have more than enough money to pay for a night in a small hotel for them both.

With so much going on in the house she decided not to panic about Tom's absence. She rang her mother-in-law and said that Priscilla thought they'd gone to London to drown their sorrows and would be back the next day.

* * *

By lunchtime there was still no sign of either of them and she was beginning to get anxious. David arrived on his bicycle mid-afternoon. The boys' half-term break was supposed to be relaxing for them and now it was anything but.

'Are you quite sure Tom didn't mention anything to you?'

'I've already told you, Babs, I didn't even know he and Jim had gone until you rang yesterday. Horrible news about Joe. Is there anything I can do to help Mrs B?'

'I've made a list of things we've now got to do. Has Grandpa spoken to you about Grandma?'

'He has. I don't think it's anything to worry about really. Don't all old people go a bit dotty?'

'Some certainly do. I'm hoping that she won't get worse for a long while. She will still be our beloved grandma whatever happens to her.'

The telephone rang at five o'clock. She was nearest so rushed to pick it up. 'The Grove, Mrs Everton speaking.'

'Hello, Babs, sorry if you've been worried about us. I'm just ringing to say that we are absolutely fine and will be back on Monday so won't miss any school.'

Before she could question him, ask him where he was, and what on earth they thought they were doing, the line went dead.

* * *

Alex landed at Holmsley South just after six in the morning. They'd been flying for just over an hour and a quarter but it seemed longer. The trucks arrived to take them for their debrief with intelligence. The three pilots that were missing weren't mentioned as they hadn't been in his flight – thank God.

Each one of them was grilled about what they'd seen and done, and the debrief took much longer than usual. For some inexplicable reason the Germans didn't seem to know the invasion had begun. The area had been heavily bombed the past twenty-four hours, which might explain why there were no troops or tanks heading for the beaches.

'Righto, chaps, well done. The wing is taking off again at 07.15. Get something to eat.'

Everybody was desperate to be included in this next wave. As a squadron leader he was given the option to join the next attack and he took it. None of the others who had been in the first show were able to go out in the second. Over the past few weeks there had been an influx of pilots – they now had more talent than they had kites.

The airfield was working at full speed, refuelling and rearming so the Typhoons would be ready for the next sortie. There was a constant stream of bombers flying overhead on their way to France.

The WAAFs were pedalling their bicycles furiously back and forth and they too seemed excited and confident that finally, after so many years, the war was going to end.

The general talk over breakfast of bacon and eggs was why the Luftwaffe hadn't arrived. 'I reckon they don't have many kites left,' someone said.

'It's more likely we caught them with their pants down. The bad weather yesterday made them think nothing was happening for a bit,' an Australian pilot said between mouthfuls.

'They don't have anything like our rocket Typhoons. We're faster than a Me109 and can outmanoeuvre them at low levels. They'll be there next time so keep your eyes peeled,' Alex said.

'You're a lucky bastard going in again, Alex. We had very little to shoot up. At least we can say we were the first in on D-Day – that's something to tell the grandkids.'

'We're working on rotation. Get a couple of hours' kip and be ready for the next show.' Alex drained his tea and headed for his billet. He just had time to use the bog and clean his teeth before returning to dispersal and doing it all over again.

This time he could see landing craft heading for the beaches, which were now criss-crossed with lethal tracers and shells. The Germans were firing from their regular gun emplacements along the coast but for some reason segments of the beach remained unscathed.

On his return he discovered that of the three pilots missing on the first show two had been picked up in the sea so that meant only one fatality. Several kites had been damaged by flak, but all were still operational. He now had four hours free. He checked his watch – almost ten o'clock. He would give Babs a ring and let her know he was safe.

He was on the way to the telephone when he was waylaid and by the time he'd dealt with the admin chappie he thought getting a few hours' kip was more important than the call. He'd fought through the Battle of Britain in his Spitfire and they'd flown sortie after sortie, had slept in their clothes on the ground whenever they got a few minutes. This was a piece of cake compared to that.

A few days later it was clear, from the map on the wall, that the Allied forces had established a bridgehead along the Normandy coast. The British army were approaching Caen and the Yanks were advancing from their own bridgeheads, of Utah and Omaha, towards the Cherbourg Peninsular.

The wing commander announced what he'd been expecting to hear. 'Things are moving on apace, chaps, and we will be operating shortly from landing strips in Normandy. I suggest that you enjoy whatever recreational time you get as there won't be any once we're in France.'

The younger members of the wing would no doubt spend every available hour downing pints of beer. Ops were now dangerous – even the most enthusiastic of the younger blokes weren't volunteering for extra duties. The Germans had moved up armoured and infantry divisions and squadrons were losing pilots steadily.

The main risk to Typhoon fighters was the flak, which was getting heavier every time they flew. On the plus side there was now a small area of friendly territory in which one could force-land without being captured by the Germans. Also, if one had to bail out in the Channel it was thick with ships and you were bound to be picked up.

He had a small window of free time and finally was able to make the call he'd intended to make when it all kicked off.

'The Grove, Mrs Everton speaking.'

'Babs, it's wonderful just to hear your voice.'

'Alex, darling, I've been so worried about you. I've got the most dreadful news. Joe was killed a few days ago. Mrs B is taking it very hard.'

'God, I'd forgotten he was likely to be at risk. I'm so sorry. Give Mrs B my love. I wish I could be there with you. How are you?'

'I'm much better. It's a bit of a struggle sometimes but I'm getting there. I'm doing all the cooking and David is being an absolute trouper...'

He detected a hesitation in her voice. There was something she wasn't telling him. 'What's up? Why isn't Tom mucking in?'

'That's the other bit of bad news. Tom and Jim went to London when they heard about Joe and they've not come back yet. They promised they would be home in time for school tomorrow.'

'They staying with friends?'

'We don't know where they are, but I don't think we have anything to worry about as they're both sensible young men.'

'Bloody hell, Babs, they're not men, they're still kids. For God's sake, can't you guess what they've done?'

'Please, don't shout at me, Alex. Grandma isn't well and I've got so much to do. I was going to involve the police if they didn't come back today.'

'It's probably too bloody late. I'm certain they've enlisted. Jim talked about doing his bit last time I was home.'

'They can't do that as they're under age.'

'They look much older – they've both been officer cadets. They know how things work. Get Edward to get on to the War Office. I'll see what I can do from this end.' He was so angry with her, so worried about the boys, that he spoke without thinking. 'I'll never forgive you if anything happens to either of them. If you'd got on to the authorities immediately...'

'Why are you being so beastly? I can't do everything. It's all very well for you – all you have to think about is killing Germans. I'm trying to hold this family together on my own.'

The line went dead and he stared at the receiver in horror. What had he done? He asked the operator to reconnect him but she told him the line was busy.

He dropped his head into his hands for a moment. What had possessed him to say something so crass? She was right – she was trying to hold the fort when she wasn't really well enough to do so. If Tom had rung her up and said he was coming back why would she have doubted that?

He spent the next hour trying to be connected to someone who was even the slightest bit interested in the fact that two boys had gone to London. Eventually he spoke to somebody who was vaguely interested.

'Squadron Leader Everton, let me assure you that there are procedures in place. If your brother and brother-in-law attempted to enlist without proof of their age they would have been turned away. You are worrying unnecessarily. Get in touch again in a few days if they haven't turned up.'

* * *

The telephone was left off the hook until Grandpa put it back a couple of hours later. She told him she must've forgotten to replace it. Babs hadn't wanted to speak to Alex but it had been a stupid thing to do as they needed to be able to receive a call from Tom. She told Grandpa what Alex had said – not the bit about never forgiving her – but that he thought the boys had gone to enlist.

'If they don't come back today then I think he might be right. If Tom had gone on his own I would be more concerned about his safety, but the likelihood of both of them being involved in such a serious mishap that they were unable to communicate with us is highly improbable.'

'I think Alex is wrong. Well, he might be right in that they have tried to enlist, but the War Office has all the soldiers they need for the invasion. I can't see them taking on anyone else at the moment, especially our boys who wouldn't be able to show their identity cards.'

'In which case, my dear, they will return eventually. I don't intend to contact the school excusing Tom's absence. He must face the music. The headmaster won't be impressed.'

'At least he's too old to get the cane but I expect they'll demote him – take away his prefect's privileges.'

'Do you think Alex will have rung his parents and told them of his suspicions?'

'He might well have done, Grandpa, so I'll call them now and hope they're not too upset.' She glanced at the grandfather clock ticking noisily in the corner of the study. 'It's eight o'clock. The boys won't be home tonight.'

The Evertons hadn't spoken to Alex, which was a relief, and like her doubted the boys would get accepted even if they were trying to enlist.

'Don't worry about it, Babs,' Grandpa said. 'They'll be back with their tails between their legs in a day or two. They'll be in hot water at school when they do appear. It serves them right for being so silly.'

'Knowing the pair of them I think it likely if they couldn't enlist in London that they will travel all over the country trying to find a recruiting office that's less efficient. I fear it might be some time before we see them again. The only good thing about this is that they sat their exams before half-term.'

'They should be starting to study for their higher certificate but I doubt missing a week or two will make much difference to them,' Grandpa assured her.

'I sincerely hope that they're not actually gone that long. It's the 12th of June today. If we haven't heard from Tom by next week then I'm going to start contacting the authorities. I know there's a war on, but they are both several years from reaching their majority. I'm going to insist that the police start looking for them.'

'Then that's what we'll do. We've got more than enough to worry about here. What were they thinking to run away and add to our stress?' Babs nodded at the phone. 'I don't want to speak to Alex if he rings up. He was absolutely beastly to me and it's going to take me a while to forgive him.'

'Put things right, my dear. Now is not the time to have arguments.'

The telephone rang, making them both jump. She hesitated and then took his advice and picked up the receiver. As she'd suspected it was Alex.

'Thank God, Babs, please don't hang up on me again. I'm sorry I shouted at you and for the things I said. I've only got a minute but I need to tell you that in the next few days the wing is relocating to Normandy. You won't be able to get in touch with me easily.'

'Thank you for telling me, but Grandpa and I think that you're wrong. The boys might want to enlist but they won't be able to – they don't have the correct papers and I doubt that the War Office is looking for new recruits just now. We don't expect them back for a week or two as they won't give up easily.'

'That's what the War Office told me. If you ring here there'll always be someone in the office – the WAAFs aren't going anywhere. A message will reach me eventually.'

She heard someone talking to him in the background. 'I can hear that you're busy. Take care, come home safe. Goodbye.' She put the receiver down wishing she'd told him that she loved him and apologised for what she'd said to him.

Life was difficult for all of them. Tom and Jim going missing so soon after Joe being killed, and then discovering that Grandma was showing signs of dementia – she just wasn't well enough to cope with all this.

She prepared a salad for supper and then put the plates on the slate shelf in the pantry where everyone could find them when they were hungry. For dessert there were strawberries and the last of the fresh cream that Ned had brought from Home Farm.

Taking her own food, plus a thermos flask of boiling water, a metal jug and two bottles for Julia, on the same tray was tricky but she didn't have the energy to make two journeys to the kitchen so she'd just have to manage.

Charlie was already asleep, thank goodness. She just needed to hold herself together long enough to feed the baby and then she would go to bed and hope that she'd feel better in the morning.

8

Alex regretted leaving things the way they were with Babs but had more pressing matters to worry about. Despite having a surplus of experienced pilots at the beginning of Operation Overlord there'd been too many casualties and now no one had more than a few hours' kip before they were out on another sortie. They were gathered together in the ops room to get the gen before the next one. This time they were to attack Panzer headquarters about twenty-five miles inland.

'Right, chaps, stay clear of the high ground as that's occupied by our troops of the 7th Armoured Division. We need to destroy these Panzer blighters as they are holding up the advance. Today you will be landing in Normandy on the new airstrip before coming back here.'

Some of the younger blokes were excited about setting foot in France and seemed to think they would be able to go out on a piss-up every night and fraternise with French girls. He didn't want to disabuse them.

The flight over was uneventful apart from avoiding the barrage balloons moored to the shipping around the coast. There was heavy cloud but they flew below it as always.

The German gunners opened fire as soon as they saw the string of Typhoons approaching. The RT crackled but none of the flyers needed telling that this was their moment to attack the château where the Germans were hiding.

They dived and hit the building and the surrounding woods with rockets and cannon shells. The raid was successful. The wing regrouped and headed for the new iron-mesh landing strip. He led them in, his squadron behind him, and he made a slow circuit of the makeshift airfield before beginning his descent.

The strip looked too short and definitely rough, but he'd landed on worse. They were surrounded on all sides by orchards and woods. The tents were dark green and almost invisible against the canopy of trees. The ack-ack positions surrounded the strip, and sandbags were piled around them to give the gunners some protection.

There was already a damaged Typhoon waiting outside a canvas maintenance hangar. This temporary building was in the middle of an orchard and the roof was quite clearly visible above the treetops.

He flew out over the coast before turning to make a circular approach towards the end of the strip. Fortunately, the undercarriages of the Typhoons were solid and withstood the heavy landing. He slammed on the brakes and rolled to a standstill and was immediately waved to a dispersal point. He recognised some of the faces as having been at Holmsley South before D-Day.

There was a constant whine of shellfire and he dived head first into the slit trenches that had been dug for the men to crouch in. A squadron remained behind but he was one of the fortunate ones and able to return to base.

There was barely time for his kite to be refuelled and rearmed before he was sent out again with another bod to destroy the blighters who'd been firing at them, pinning them in the trenches and making them have to take off under fire.

The mission was successful and he hoped in future things would be less hairy for all of them. The plan was to fly out first thing, rearm and refuel on the temporary base in Normandy, and then return to England after ops were over.

It was several days before he had a moment to ring home. Edward answered the phone.

'Have the boys been in contact?' There wasn't time for idle chatter as there was a queue of men desperate to use the telephone after him. He no longer had access to the office as it was filled with senior officers of all sorts.

'No, but Jim rang your parents on Tuesday. He told them they were trying to enlist and were heading for Kent in the hope they could persuade someone to take them on.'

'That's a remote possibility, thank God. At least we know they're safe. Give Babs and the children my love.'

He handed the telephone to the bloke behind him, wishing it had been his beloved girl who'd picked up the phone. He was too knackered to do more than stagger to his billet, strip off and head for the shower with a towel wrapped around his waist.

The pattern of his days continued. On Friday he almost went for a Burton. The fuselage was riddled with holes and he barely made it back to base.

'There ain't any others for you to take, sir, and I reckon it's going to take a week to patch this one up.'

He thanked the ground crew, staggered into the waiting truck and returned for the debrief.

'Squadron Leader Everton, sir, the CO needs like to speak to you immediately.' The WAAF who'd spoken saluted and he followed her.

One look at his commanding officer's face and he knew it was bad news. 'Sit down, old boy, I've the worst possible news. Your brother, Jim, was killed in London on Tuesday by a flying bomb. Your brother-in-law, Tom, escaped the explosion with minor injuries and is now back home.'

Alex swallowed the lump in his throat. For some reason his response was to ask how many casualties there had been.

'Eight dead, a dozen injured. The most appalling bad luck for the boys to be crossing the railway bridge at Mile End when the bloody thing came down. There's a Moth waiting to take you to Hornchurch. I expect you can get a lift home from there.'

'My kite's out of action for a week. I'll take it as compassionate leave.'

As he was still in his flight suit, travelling in an open cockpit was no problem. Half an hour later he was airborne, still unable to process the fact that his brother had been killed in such an arbitrary way. He shouldn't even have been in Mile End – he should have been at school.

Instead of going to The Grove he went straight to Home Farm. His parents would be devastated, Ned also. They needed him more than Babs and the children did.

* * *

'Why didn't Alex come here first? I don't understand why he went to his parents without calling in to see us.'

'Babs, my dear girl, your brother is still alive – a bit battered and grief-stricken, but still here. Jim is dead. Of course he's going to go to offer what comfort he can to his family,' Grandpa said.

Grandma had taken Mrs B to stay with friends somewhere in the wilds of Suffolk, away from the constant reminder of the war.

She didn't even know that Jim had died. Heaven knows how either of them would deal with that news when they did return.

This meant that everything was now resting on her shoulders. Grandpa had visibly aged overnight and David was spending every minute with his brother. They were both inconsolable about the loss of their friend and she could hardly ask them to put their own feelings aside and help her.

She now had the added task of taking care of the horses, feeding the chickens, dogs and cat, as well as everything else she was already doing. Alex should have come back. She needed him more than his parents did. They had plenty of help – she was buckling under the weight of it all.

David had told her Alex had a week's compassionate leave. There wouldn't be a funeral. There were no recognisable remains to bury. The thought was just too ghastly and she could imagine the pain the family were in. Her brother had witnessed his best friend being blown to smithereens. He wouldn't recover from such a thing easily.

Four days after David had told her that Alex was back, he finally turned up. He now had just one day left of his leave. She was exhausted mentally and physically and thought his absence unforgivable. Even Grandpa now considered her husband had let them all down badly.

If Alex had expected to be greeted warmly, to be offered sympathy and tea, he was sadly disappointed. She stared at him coldly as did her grandfather.

'Are we supposed to be grateful that you bothered to put in an appearance at all, Alex? We could understand you going to Home Farm first, but your duty was to your own family. We needed you here.'

She was holding the baby in her arms. Charlie was standing

beside her. She expected her son to rush to his daddy but he remained where he was.

Alex dropped to his haunches and held out his arms to his son but the little boy didn't budge.

'Go to your daddy, Charlie. He's come to see us.' She gave him a gentle nudge and reluctantly he sidled forward but without his usual enthusiasm. The past few days had been horrible but too late she realised she and Grandpa had talked too freely in front of him and much of it not very complimentary about Alex. This was as unforgivable as him not coming sooner.

'We'll leave you to talk to Charlie, Alex. Come through to the kitchen when you've finished. I've got to feed Julia.'

He joined them after a few minutes and Charlie immediately ran to her side and pressed himself against her. One look at the kitchen, the debris on the table, the unwashed floor should show Alex just how bad things had been.

Grandpa was pouring tea into mugs and had his back to them. Alex pulled out a chair at the other side of the table and sat down. He looked defeated, exhausted and she wanted to put things right between them but instead tears trickled down her cheeks. She ignored them. The baby whimpered as her arms tightened involuntarily.

'I'm sorry about Jim. Tom's not come down since he got back and neither has David. Mrs B and Grandma are staying in Suffolk and don't even know what happened.' She couldn't say any more. Talking was becoming impossible.

Grandpa put down the tea in front of her and pushed a handkerchief into her hand. Alex was still hunched in the chair, staring at the table.

'Babs is buckling under the strain, Alex. I thought better of you.'

At Grandpa's words her husband raised his head. 'How the hell was I supposed to know what was happening here if you didn't bother to tell me? All you had to do was pick up the telephone and ask.'

Babs wiped her eyes and put the half-empty bottle on the table. She then laid Julia over her shoulder and began patting her back. This gave her a few moments to gather her thoughts. He was right – they could have telephoned but they shouldn't have had to.

'I expected you to come as soon as you'd spoken to your parents. Why didn't you ring us? Did you really think that Tom and David would be in any fit state to do anything but grieve?' The baby belched, the sound loud and incongruous in the heavy silence. Charlie had climbed onto Grandpa's lap, put his thumb in his mouth and fallen asleep. He was doing that a lot lately.

'I'll go up and see them.' Alex ignored his tea, pushed himself to his feet as if he was an old man, and walked out.

She didn't have the energy to go after him but knew that she should if she wanted to mend the growing rift between them. If Charlie hadn't been sitting on Grandpa, she could have handed the baby to him. Instead, she continued to cry silently as she fed Julia, knowing she should be talking to Alex but unable to do so.

When he came down and she could put the baby in her pram, she would insist that Alex came outside in the garden with her. It was always easier to talk in the fresh air. He was risking his life several times a day and deserved better from her. His actions had been thoughtless, but she didn't want him to leave without them both having a chance to apologise.

'Alex has been upstairs a long time, Grandpa. I hope Tom will feel a bit better after talking to him. I'll put Julia down and carry Charlie into the sitting room. He can sleep on the sofa. Would you mind keeping an eye on both of them whilst I go upstairs?'

'Go ahead, my dear, and leave the boy here. He's comfortable and so am I. If he urinates it's better on me and the kitchen floor than on the sofa.'

As she approached the nursery floor she'd expected to hear voices, but it was quiet. She ran up the last flight and pushed open the boys' bedroom door. They were both asleep and there was no sign of Alex. She could hardly wake them to ask so rushed back downstairs.

He'd probably gone outside to see what he could do to help – better late than never. Fortunately, they still had a small acreage of meadow that hadn't been ploughed up to grow vegetables and both horses were turned out.

She called his name but it echoed without response around the stable yard. Her heart began to pound, and a sick feeling settled in her stomach. After a further ten minutes of frantic calling and searching she realised that Alex had gone. He'd not even bothered to come in and say goodbye. Not considered her feelings. Not tried to put things right – he'd just walked out.

She slumped against the wall and slowly her legs folded until she was sitting on the cobbles. Was this the end of her marriage? Could she ever forgive him for abandoning his family so callously? She tried to rationalise her grief and anger. He was a fighter pilot, no doubt flying constant sorties without respite and, on top of that, he'd received dreadful news. He wasn't thinking straight. When he'd recovered, he would get in touch and apologise and she would do the same.

Yes – she was overreacting. Their marriage had already been through so much and remained strong so they would get over this, given time. She would ring Home Farm and speak to him there. He still had another day of compassionate leave so there was time to put things right before he had to return.

She just couldn't let him go like this. He needed to be on top form to stay alive. After all, Charlie had only been conceived because she hadn't wanted to tell John she didn't love him and had only been engaged to him so he would go away to war happy.

* * *

Alex was bouncing about in the back of an army truck when, instead of feeling sorry for himself, he understood what his actions, or lack of them, had meant to his darling girl. The lorry lurched to a halt outside Hornchurch. It had taken him three hours to get this far.

He scrambled out and thanked the driver. He couldn't go back now. It was too late and he was committed to returning to his base. This whole thing was a bloody shambles and a lot of it his fault. He reported to the adjutant and was told there would be a taxi Anson to take him to his base in a couple of hours. This gave him ample time to find a telephone and try and put things right with Babs. He also had to reclaim his flight gear and chute, which he'd left in a spare locker a few days ago.

'Alex, old bean, I didn't expect to see you again.' Binky Forsyth, one of the men he had been incarcerated with, threw his arms around him.

He returned the embrace. 'Bloody hell, Binky, are you stationed here?'

'I'd hardly be at Hornchurch if I wasn't. I was transferred here just after your move to Holmsley South. Have you come back to join us?'

The telephone call was forgotten in the pleasure of the reunion and by the time he remembered it was too late and his taxi was waiting. Reminiscing with Binky had meant he could forget his grief for a while.

'When this lot's over, if we haven't kicked the bucket, we'll get together. Sorry about your brother, old bean. Horrible way to go.'

This time they just shook hands vigorously and made promises to keep in touch. In the short flip home, he pushed aside his misery at the death of his brother, at quite possibly losing his wife and children, and focused his mind on what he had to do. He would concentrate on staying alive, on not taking any unnecessary risks, and pray that when the war was over, he still had a home and family to go back to.

* * *

Over the next few weeks Babs began to accept that Alex no longer wanted to be part of the family. If he did, then he would have at least written to her, rung her up occasionally, but since he'd walked out she'd heard nothing from him.

In late June her sister-in-law, Valerie, had a little boy and they called him James after his uncle who was no longer with them. Things were very strained between her and the Evertons, but at least Ned and David remained firm friends.

Tom refused to return to school. He'd cut off all contact with his former friends and also with Priscilla. After a month the principal had expelled him. When the letter had arrived her brother had been pleased.

'It wouldn't be the same without Jim. Nothing will ever be the same. He was my best friend...'

She'd been tiptoeing around him, made no demands on him despite the extra work it meant that she and David had to do. Finally, she lost her temper.

'Stop feeling sorry for yourself, Tom. What happened was dreadful, but hundreds of thousands of people have lost their lives in this war and their families and friends don't mope around the house making a nuisance of themselves. Do you think Jim would want you to give up your dreams of becoming a doctor because he died?'

He recoiled and his mouth opened and shut like he was a

stranded fish for a few moments. 'You don't understand...' he muttered.

'I understand perfectly. Did I give up when I thought that Alex was dead? Have I given up now even though my husband has left me?' No sooner had she spoken the words than she regretted them. This was between her and Alex and she'd no wish to involve the family in her marital problems.

Tom's face crumpled. He no longer looked like a young man but a grief-stricken child. She held out her arms and he threw himself into them. He was now a head taller than her and she guided him to the sofa so she could comfort him more easily.

He cried, great wrenching sobs, for some time before gulping to a stop. Grandpa, as always, appeared with his handkerchief and pushed it into his grandson's hand.

Tom sat up, blew his nose and mopped his eyes. 'I'm so sorry, Babs. I didn't know that you and Alex had split up. Was it because of me?' His voice shook and fresh tears filled his eyes. 'Jim wouldn't be dead if we hadn't gone to London. Now I've ruined your life as well.'

'Don't be ridiculous. I didn't mean to say anything about Alex. It's got nothing to do with you, not really. I've not been well or I would have dealt with things better.'

'I'll be okay now. It needed you to shake me out of my self-pity. Do you think if I go cap in hand Brentwood will take me back?'

'I'm sure they will. Go in with David tomorrow and speak to the headmaster.'

'It's a good thing that Mrs B and Grandma haven't been here to see me like this. Do they even know about Jim?'

'Yes, Grandpa wrote to them. Mrs B is now ready to come back and resume her duties. I think I'd better tell you that Grandma is getting a little confused and is not herself. That's why we thought it a good idea that she stayed in Suffolk until things calmed down here.'

'I'll give the kitchen a good clean, scrub the floors and so on. I reckon I can get everything shipshape before David gets back from school. Unless there's something else you'd rather I did?'

'No, that would be absolutely splendid. I was rather dreading having to spring-clean the place over the next couple of days. I couldn't let Mrs B and Grandma come back with it looking like a tip.'

'Hardly as bad as that, my dear, and I'm sure that both of them would understand in the circumstances.' Grandpa came in with a tray of much-needed tea and for the first time since Joe had died Babs began to feel things might one day be bearable.

9

Alex was still not based permanently in Normandy but the move was imminent, so he was told. He was flying constant sorties, leaving him no time to do anything but grab something to eat and a couple of hours' sleep before taking off again. The only good thing about this was that he didn't worry about Babs, Jim or anything else.

The push forward by the Yanks and the British had stalled – the chaps thought the brown jobs should get their fingers out. Ten days after Jim had died so horribly he was on a mission to destroy the dug-in tanks along the side of the road, which were apparently the reason why the armies weren't moving forward as planned.

He dived towards the target, knowing that range was crucial. The rockets were most accurate at around a mile. He was preparing to fire when he saw the puffs of smoke coming from the Typhoon in front of him, indicating this chap had already fired. Alex released his eight rockets, pulled out of his dive and into an almost vertical climb.

The pressure from the G-force was so intense he was unable to move and greyed out. Being semi-conscious often happened to a pilot when coming out of a steep dive and he'd become used to the unpleasant sensation.

The bloke who'd attacked with him appeared at his side and grinned and waved. For some reason he repeatedly put his wing inside Alex's and was edging closer and closer. The little bastard's antics meant he couldn't relax after the attack and when he landed he headed straight for the idiot.

'What the hell were you playing at? First you pull out so late from your dive you could have been killed and then played silly buggers on the way back. This is war – not the bloody Hendon air display.'

He immediately regretted his outburst. It wasn't just battle fatigue – he needed to sort out his personal life before he did something worse than snarl at a fellow pilot.

He could have found the time to ring over the past weeks even if it had meant giving up eating or sleeping. He was putting it off because he didn't want to know for certain that he and Babs were permanently estranged.

This was a conversation he needed to have without a queue of blokes behind him listening to every word. He marched straight into the office. There were two army officers in situ.

'I need to make a private call. Can I have the room for a bit, if you don't mind?' They were both majors so were of equal rank, which made things easier.

'Go ahead, the room's all yours,' one of them said with a friendly smile.

Alex snatched up the receiver, dialled, gave the number and waited to be connected. His knuckles gleamed white around the telephone.

'The Grove, Mrs Sinclair speaking.'

'Elspeth, how are you? I've only got a few minutes and I desperately need to speak to Babs. Would you fetch her for me?' He'd not given her a chance to answer his polite enquiry but there wasn't time to fuss about such niceties.

'I'm glad that you're still in the land of the living, young man. I did wonder.'

There was a rattle as the receiver was put down on the desk, the clip-clip of Elspeth's court shoes on the boards and then voices in the distance. Then he heard running footsteps. The weight on his chest began to lift a little. It must be a good sign if she was hurrying to take his call.

'Alex, I'm so glad you called. Tom's a lot better and has gone back to school. Mrs B has taken back the reins of the household – thank goodness – and Grandma hasn't got any worse. How are you? It must be almost four weeks since you left without saying goodbye.'

There was something missing from her voice. She didn't sound like the same woman. She was talking to him as if he was a friend, someone she was quite fond of, but not the man she loved. 'I'm so sorry, Babs. I've no excuse for the way I behaved. You should understand that I wasn't myself at the time. You were all over the place after you had the baby, remember?'

There was a long pause before she answered. 'Yes, that's a fair point, Alex. I was suffering from a medical condition. What's your excuse? I still stayed with my family, however difficult it was. I didn't abandon my children the way that you abandoned us.'

'Don't be like that, Babs. I was grieving, confused...'

She interrupted him. 'So were we all. You should have put your own feelings to one side and helped us. Isn't the man of the house supposed to be looking after those in his care?'

'I've apologised. What must I do to put things right between us?'

'It's been nearly a month since you walked out without a word. If you found time to ring me now you could have done so weeks ago. You've left it too late, Alex. I'm not sure how I feel about you any more. Maybe in time I'll try and forgive you as you are my husband and the father of one of my children. Thank you for calling. Take care. Goodbye.'

The line went dead. The father of one of her children. The words echoed in his head and he wanted to smash the telephone against the wall. Charlie was legally his son. He loved him as much as he loved his daughter and wasn't going to give him up. He straightened and came to a decision. This situation was his fault but she had no grounds for divorce and he didn't intend to give her any.

His fountain pen and stationery folder were in his billet. He was going to write to her immediately and make sure it went in the post today.

His orderly fetched him a pile of sandwiches, two mugs of tea and a bun. 'Can't let you go hungry, sir. Don't want you fainting from lack of food, now do we?'

'I've got a letter to write, then I'm going to crash out. Will you stick it in the post box for me later?'

'Roger that, Skip.'

This was going to be the most difficult letter he'd ever written. Somehow, he had to make Babs understand that whatever had happened they belonged together, that he loved her and the children and wasn't going to give up on their marriage.

* * *

Over the weeks since she'd last seen Alex, Babs had tried to get on with being a mother, sister and granddaughter to the best of her ability. She'd made a dreadful hash of being a wife and thought she possibly wasn't cut out for this role.

Receiving his telephone call had been a shock. Why had he suddenly decided to contact her? What had changed for him? She wasn't sure if she was pleased to hear from him or if this just made things harder. Charlie had stopped asking when his daddy was coming to see him because Tom and David had explained to him that Alex was busy fighting the Germans and would be home when the war was won.

The Grove was running smoothly once more. Mrs B was subdued but just as efficient as she always had been. Tom was equally quiet, but even more determined to become a doctor eventually. Grandma was happy enough and if she did forget things occasionally so far it hadn't been anything critical.

'Babs, my dear, what did that reprehensible young man have to say after ignoring you for so long?' Grandpa had arrived at her side.

'He apologised and said that he wants to put things right. I couldn't think of anything encouraging to say to him. I never doubted that I loved him all the time he was missing and I don't know why I can't say the words any more. I will welcome him back when the war's over and must simply hope things will gradually get back to the way they were.'

'I can think of one reason why you've taken a step back from your relationship. You went through hell when he was shot down, declared dead, and I think you're subconsciously protecting yourself from what might happen.' Grandpa squeezed her hand. 'You've convinced yourself that you don't love him just in case he's killed.'

'I can't believe that's true. Just the thought of him used to make me feel tingly all over. Now I merely think of him in the same way that I used to think of John. The spark's gone. Actually, I think this is more to do with me than him. I don't feel like a complete woman. Intimacy was designed to produce children and now I can't have them I've gone off the whole idea.'

'Early days, my dear girl, early days. Just take one day at a time, enjoy the company of your delightful children and don't worry about the future. Things have a way of working out in the end.'

She sighed and smiled sadly. 'It's been such a horrible few

weeks and I don't think I'm the same person I was before. On another subject entirely, Grandpa, I think it's a shame David's no longer invited over to Home Farm. We should be asked to visit as well. Julia's an actual Everton, even if Charlie isn't...'

'That's quite enough of that nonsense, my girl. I don't want to hear you say anything like that ever again. Charlie is as much an Everton as his sister as far as everyone else's concerned.'

'Remember, John threatened to come here and reveal the secret. He could still do that, and that's another thing that's been playing on my mind.'

'Have you spoken to him since that phone call?'

She shook her head.

'Then I think it might be a good idea to write to him. Probably easier than speaking to him in person. Tell him that your son isn't anything to do with him, that he hasn't a legal leg to stand on, that we will all deny his accusations if he makes any.'

'That's all very well, Grandpa, but I think if you put the two of them in the same room it would be impossible to deny that John's his biological father.'

'Then we'll just have to make absolutely certain John doesn't come here. I would suggest that you sever all links with him, however fond you are of his parents; it will be better that way. Charlie has the same colouring as your brothers and there's no mistaking their relationship. That should be sufficient if John did decide to make trouble for you.'

'I'll write the letter tonight. Will you read it for me before I send it? I don't want to say the wrong thing and make matters even worse.'

She no longer listened to the nine o'clock news. The doodlebugs continued to fall on London with devastating consequences. Every time she heard about one dropping it brought back Jim's death. If there was anything significant that she should know then Grandpa gave her an edited version in the morning.

Once the children were safely asleep she sat at her desk and prepared to write what was going to be the most difficult letter she'd ever written. She'd had to write to John before and break off the engagement. This was going to be far worse, as if she didn't get it right, he could turn up on the doorstep and ruin everything. Not only for Charlie, but also for the Evertons who obviously believed him to be their grandson.

Dear John,

I'm sorry to have to write such a difficult letter to you but after your threats when you telephoned a few months ago I believe I have no option.

Since then Joe, Mrs B's son, was killed in Normandy. Then Jim Everton, Alex's brother, was killed in London by the first doodlebug that dropped.

You will see how this changes everything. Mr and Mrs Everton have lost a precious son. They already lost a granddaughter a few years ago, and I'll not allow them to be upset by your accusations.

My son is an Everton. Alex is his father. I'll just say these are the ramblings of a man with a damaged mind.

You were my best friend whilst I was growing up. I couldn't have survived the abuse I received from my mother without the love and support of you and your family. I shall always be grateful for that. However, your behaviour has changed things.

You are a good man. I think the trauma of your dreadful accident, the break-up of your engagement and the amount that you're drinking is making you say and do things that are out of character.

I'm certain that you won't want to upset your parents and cause further unpleasantness.

I don't love you; I never have – not in the way you wanted me to. It's time for you to forget about me and move on with your life. I shall not be communicating with you or your parents again.

Best wishes,

Barbara Everton

* * *

Alex tore up his first three attempts to write to Babs. The fourth he thought was as good as it was going to get.

Darling Babs,

I wish I could hold you in my arms and speak to you rather than having to write this letter. I'll start by apologising again for not doing what I should have done, for not being the husband I should have been.

It broke my heart when you said that Charlie wasn't my son. He is in every way that matters. Whatever you might think I don't care that we can't have any more children. I do care that things went so disastrously wrong when Julia was born and that it's made you sad.

I love you. I've loved you from the first moment I met you all those years ago. Loving you is what kept me alive during those months I was trying to get home. Whatever you decide, I'll always love you. I'll do anything you want in order to put things right.

I'll understand if you no longer want to share a bed with me. As long as I can come home when this bloody war's over, can be a father to our children, a help to Edward and Elspeth, a friend and mentor to your brothers, then I'll settle for that.

I've let you down but I'll make it up to you if you give me the chance.

All my love forever,

Alex

Alex read it through for the umpteenth time and then decided it would do. He only had an hour before he was back on duty. He didn't bother to undress just flopped back on the bed, closed his eyes and was instantly asleep.

His orderly roused him with a much-needed cuppa. Strange how even when the weather was hot, tea was still welcome. He dunked his head in a sink full of cold water, cleaned his teeth and headed for the ops room along with everyone else.

Today was the day they were transferring the remainder of the wing to the temporary base in Normandy. The facilities there were basic – no shower, no nothing, really. He would have to wash in a canvas bowl, sleep in a tent on a camp bed.

After the briefing the Canadian bloke, not known as Ace for nothing, told Alex that if he wanted action he should stay with him. They were drifting along enjoying the sunshine when Ace's voice came over the RT telling them he'd seen something.

Alex followed in a steep dive but seeing tracer bullets heading straight for him heaved on the stick in an attempt to avoid being killed. There was a hideous pain in his guts and he blacked out. He came round to discover he was climbing rapidly.

When he tried to move his hands to throttle back, he couldn't do it. He must've been hit. If he didn't do something the kite would stall and he'd go for a Burton. An image of Babs flashed into his head and somehow he was able to kick the rudder and drift to the side and stop climbing.

Ace was calling him but he couldn't answer. His arms refused to work. Any movement increased the agony in his stomach. Gradually the pain lessened and he finally felt life returning to his limbs.

His landing was rough but at least he was down without a prang. He couldn't scramble out of the cockpit and had to be helped. The doc was waiting and he was carted ignominiously on a stretcher to the hospital tent.

After he was prodded and poked in the guts he was pronounced undamaged. He'd left his stomach behind when he'd pulled out of the dive so suddenly and it was going to take a couple of days for him to get back into shape.

'Grounded for two days, Squadron Leader.'

This was bad news for any flyer. Alex wished he'd managed to drag himself out of the cockpit and avoided being seen by the medic. He was driven back to the tents and, still sore, found it difficult to get out of the jeep, much to the amusement of his flight.

'Bloody hell, we thought you were a goner. Glad to have you back,' someone said with a grin.

'Ace came back full of holes; the flak was fearsome today.'

Alex had panicked. There was no excuse for someone of his experience doing something so stupid. He left his mates chatting and walked to his tent, wincing with every step. He wouldn't have pulled out like that if his mind had been fully on the job. From now on he was going to concentrate wholeheartedly on staying alive. He was determined to get back to his family eventually.

10

Babs didn't open Alex's letter immediately. Instead, she put it, with the others he'd written to her, in a drawer on her dressing table. She wasn't ready to read it yet. After posting the letter to John she'd been on edge expecting him to telephone, write or – even worse – appear in person to dispute her decision.

Her brothers broke up for the summer holidays. Tom had received his school certificate having achieved distinction in every subject. The Evertons were given Jim's certificate posthumously and this brought back the sadness left by his death.

'Babs, I've got a job as a porter at the hospital in Brentwood. I need to get some experience if I'm going to get into Oxford next year to study medicine.'

'Well done. I'm proud of you. When do you start?'

'Tomorrow. I'll cycle in. My shift starts at seven thirty and finishes twelve hours later.'

'Golly, you'll be exhausted when you get back. Which days do you have off?'

'None. It's only for six weeks. Don't look so horrified, Sis, I'm a big boy now. Alex doesn't get any days off, does he? He's risking his life every day as well.'

'Good heavens! That reminds me I had a letter from him weeks ago and I've not read it yet. I'd forgotten all about it.'

Tom frowned. 'Are things okay with you and Alex now? Did you make up?'

She was tempted to lie but decided if her brother was old enough to work then he deserved the truth. 'No, things are not good. We both said things we shouldn't have and I'm just not sure how I feel about him any more.'

'Are you getting a divorce?'

'Of course not. I'm sure we'll sort things out once he's home again for good. He's part of this family and always will be.'

'You won't find anyone better – that's for sure. John was never right for you. I don't understand why Mr and Mrs Everton don't want to see their grandchildren. Even if they blame us for Jim's death, it's got nothing to do with Charlie and Julia.'

'I know it's not fair. They must think that we could have done more to find you both, that it isn't fair you survived and Jim was killed. Things have never been the same since little Judith died. I've tried ringing but Alex's mother made it quite clear she didn't want to hear from me again. Thank goodness we've got our grandpa and grandma to make a fuss of them both.'

'They've also got two besotted uncles, Mrs B and yourself to dote on them. They're not missing out.'

She hugged her brother and he wandered off to find Ned and David who were somewhere outside in the grounds doing something useful.

David no longer went to Home Farm but Ned still spent all his free time at The Grove. He was now working on the farm and no doubt would be busy most days during the holidays.

Once the house was quiet Babs recovered the letter she'd

ignored and opened it. She was in tears when she'd finished and bitterly regretted the fact that she hadn't opened it at once. Alex was now stationed in France but he said if she wrote to Holmsley South it would eventually reach him.

Dearest Alex,

I was still cross with you when your letter arrived and put it to one side and then completely forgot about it until now.

I'm so sorry I didn't reply. You've nothing to apologise for. We both behaved badly. I should never have said that Charlie wasn't your son.

I wrote to John telling him I wanted no further contact with him and that we'd all deny he had anything to do with Charlie if he started causing problems.

I miss you dreadfully and so do the children. I do love you but knowing you don't expect me to sleep with you is a great relief. I just don't seem to have those sorts of feelings any longer.

I hope you are keeping safe and not taking any risks. Tom did very well and got his certificate. It broke all our hearts that Jim would also have got his if he'd still been here.

Your parents don't want anything to do with our children or me. However, Ned is ignoring the embargo and comes over to stay every week.

Tom has got a job as a porter at the hospital. He is quite determined to follow in Grandpa's footsteps and become a doctor one day.

Julia is very advanced. She is trying to crawl now, sitting up on her own and joins us for meals in the high chair.

I know you can't write to me but I'll write again in a week or two and let you know how we're all doing.

I love you,

Your Babs

She blotted the letter, written on the flimsy almost transparent airmail paper, carefully folded it and put it in the envelope. Tom could post it when he pedalled past the post office tomorrow morning. Fortunately, she had a stamp to stick on it.

After checking the children, a nightly routine, she retired and prayed that the letter didn't take too long to reach Alex. She woke with a jolt a few hours later not sure what had woken her. She sat up and listened. The telephone wasn't ringing – thank God – as that would mean the worst possible news. The children were quiet, so was the house.

She was about to settle down again when she heard movement on the stairs. The hairs on the back of her neck stood up. Were they being burgled?

No – that was silly because the dogs would be barking. She was wide awake and sitting up listening carefully. The footsteps were definitely coming up the stairs not going down, which was a bit of a worry. She slipped out of bed, tiptoed to the door and opened it. It was totally dark so whoever was creeping about didn't have a torch.

'Who is it? What are you doing out there?'

Whoever it was said something very rude and there was the sound of a person falling backwards down the narrow stairs. The racket was enough to wake the dead and certainly enough to wake both Julia and Charlie who started to cry. Then Grandpa appeared in his pyjamas with his hair standing on end. He'd had the forethought to switch on his bedroom light.

Then she laughed. 'That's Tom. I do hope he didn't hurt himself.'

Her brother's voice echoed up the staircase. 'I could have broken my neck, Babs. What were you thinking to burst out of your bedroom and frighten me to death?' He sounded a bit odd and for a moment she thought he was injured.

'He's drunk, Babs. He must have sneaked off somewhere after you thought he was asleep.'

'In which case, Grandpa, I'll leave you to deal with him. I suppose it's only fair if he's going to do a man's job that he should be allowed to have a few drinks.'

'I'll make him a strong coffee. We were saving it for a special occasion and I think this qualifies. Elspeth took a sleeping draught so would sleep through a hurricane. Go and see to the little ones. I'll see to Thomas.'

Julia had already gone back to sleep but Charlie refused to settle down. 'I was very scared, Mummy. I want to come in your bed tonight.'

'You can come in for half an hour and then I'll take you back. It was your Uncle Tom falling down the stairs but he hasn't hurt himself.'

'What's drunk mean, Mummy?'

'It means that Tom had some beer and it made him silly. Grandpa will look after him.'

'I want some beer so I can be silly.'

She hugged her little boy. 'You are quite silly enough without drinking any beer, young man.'

***

A week after the losing his stomach incident, Alex was grounded once again and this time through no fault of his own. For some stupid reason no one had thought to fit filters on the engines and they were now packing up on a regular basis as the dust from the rudimentary airstrip got sucked in.

Some clever sod had rigged up a shower using a bucket with holes in it and a piece of string. After a few teething problems when the entire bucket of water had fallen on the unfortunate man standing underneath, they'd got it working properly.

It was an ingenious contraption and there were now half a dozen of them dotted about the camp. He certainly felt better being able to get clean all over. Nobody bothered to shave every day, but they still looked reasonable.

'Oi, Skip, there's a letter for you,' someone yelled as he was waving the pale blue envelope above his head.

It could be a letter from his mother, but he doubted it, so with any luck it was an answer from Babs after all this time. He took it to his tent, which fortunately was empty. He sat on the camp bed and looked at it. Definitely Babs's writing. Bloody hell – his hands were shaking.

He was careful opening the flimsy envelope as he didn't want to tear the contents. He closed his eyes, sent up a quick prayer and then opened the paper.

By the time he got to the bottom he was a new man. She'd forgiven him. She loved him and she'd sent John packing. The news couldn't be better. He looked at the date – it had been written only a week ago so had been forwarded from Holmsley South with commendable speed.

After scrabbling about in his locker he found his fountain pen and something to write on. Not airmail paper, but anything would do. His kite was out of action today so he would write to Babs and also to his mother. It wasn't right that Charlie and Julia no longer saw their grandparents.

This letter was far easier to write than the previous one. He told Babs about losing his stomach, about his kite being grounded, about the makeshift showers but didn't mention the awful loss of life in the wing. By the time he was demobbed his daughter might well be walking. He'd be a stranger to her – but some of the poor sods had been away for the duration. He smiled wryly. Any babies born to their wives wouldn't be theirs and would be an unwelcome shock.

A few of the blokes had been seriously shot up, received basic first aid from the doctor on the base, and had then been shipped home to Blighty.

The only good thing about being in Normandy was that all the flyers knew they were doing a damn good job and their efforts were saving lives, possibly thousands. The Luftwaffe had never appeared in any numbers. Those bloody doodlebugs continued to drop on London, killing hundreds despite the fact that the launch sites were continually being bombed.

Rome had been liberated in June and from what he'd heard Paris would be next. The French were lucky – their capital city hadn't been bombed much, unlike London. He put none of this in either of the letters.

He stuffed both letters into envelopes, added the addresses, and strolled across to the admin tent to hand them in. No stamps were needed at this end.

* * *

July merged into August. They had been at Le Fresne for six weeks now. Relentless flying of sorties had reduced the numbers of both pilots and kites available at any one time. There was a steady influx of new blokes and by August his squadron was almost unrecognisable. They were to move eighty miles to the south-east of Le Fresne, sixty miles west of Paris and almost due south of Rouen.

Hauling the heavy Typhoon in and out of dives and climbs was hard work. Alex longed to be back at Hornchurch flying his beloved Spitfires but he had to do whatever was asked of him. There was no chance of getting home leave every six to eight weeks as he had when based in England.

One night he lay on his camp bed listening to people talking on the other side of the hedge. They were the ground crew preparing to run the Sabre engines to make sure they were functioning as they should. They never had this problem with Spitfires.

He missed Babs and the children, was still grieving for his brother, and the constant loss of men from his squadron was just adding to his misery. Of the original twelve in his squadron there were only himself and two others. All the rest had bought it.

Dwelling on what he couldn't change wasn't helping him and certainly wouldn't help his fellow pilots. He had something to live for, something to go home to, and he was going to do his damnedest to stay alive until he could be back with his family.

* * *

The brown jobs were moving fast through the Low Countries towards Antwerp, so another move was imminent. His squadron was briefed to make an armed recce at a place called Charleville-Mézières. Alex stacked his camp bed as well as his personal belongings into the gun bay of his Typhoon.

'This looks more like it, Alex. Vitry airfield is close to Douai. I reckon there'll be bars and girls available,' one of his squadron said happily.

'Let's hope so. It seems a long time since we had any fun. The Met officer has warned of storms in our target area.' He stared up into the cloudless sky. 'Nothing here, but he's not often wrong.'

He led his squadron low across the fields in open formation but they found nothing. They'd been searching in circles for some time when they flew into the centre of an electrical storm. His compass spun wildly and all he got on the RT was static. It was impossible to fly in close formation in heavy cloud and turbulence as the kite was being tossed from side to side like a ship in a storm.

None of the blokes would know where they were and would be relying on him to find somewhere safe to land. Finally, Alex burst through the cloud into clear blue sky and sunlight and tried to work out his position. They'd been airborne for an hour and forty minutes and were dangerously low on fuel.

The whole sortie had been a waste of time as they'd seen nothing to shoot at. They would have to force-land on the wrong side of the lines. Not a happy thought.

The tail-end Charlie's engine began to cough and splutter just as Alex saw a large airfield with long runways damaged by bomb craters. There were German aircraft lined up on the apron outside the headquarters area.

The place looked deserted but they couldn't land on the runways. 'There's a grass area beside the main hangars – we'll have to land there.' Alex had no idea if there were still Germans on the airfield but they had no choice as they were all out of fuel.

There were labourers in the surrounding fields who saw the Typhoons circling and they mistakenly believed they were being liberated from the Germans.

One after the other the kites landed, narrowly missing the pylons around the perimeter. They parked on the grass opposite the main hangar. They were all delighted to be down safely as landing a Typhoon with no fuel wasn't fun.

He beckoned the others to join him. 'We're behind the lines and I don't know how far away the Germans are. Keep your revolvers ready just in case. Put a bullet through your petrol tank if there's trouble.'

'Where the hell are we, Skip?' his second in command, Billy, asked.

'Haven't the foggiest. We've just got to hope that someone notices an entire squadron is missing and comes to look for us.' He noticed one of the blokes had climbed up on the wing of a

Heinkel and was about to open the cabin door. 'Get off, you blithering idiot, it'll be booby-trapped.' Alex's shout echoed across the empty airfield and with an embarrassed shrug Archie jumped down.

Before they could do anything else a crowd of French women suddenly appeared on the edge of the airfield and were running towards them waving their arms and shouting in welcome.

'Bloody hell, they think we've come to liberate them. Just smile and say nothing,' Alex said.

His French was okay and he tried to explain that they'd landed because they'd run out of fuel but these ladies didn't listen. Babies were held up to be kissed and they had no option but to go along with it.

Some of the women dragged trestle tables out from the hangar and black bread, cheese and jugs of wine were produced and an impromptu liberation party was held. A member of the French Resistance, a gun slung over his shoulder, approached Alex.

The man beamed. Alex thought he asked when the British tanks would be arriving and that he was surprised the RAF had got there first. Alex replied that he was surprised too and then walked away quickly before he would be forced to own up to what had actually happened.

As he was munching bread and cheese and drinking a mug of decent red wine, he took Billy to one side. 'We just have to hope that someone will spot us and send the brown jobs in with fuel so we can get away.'

'From what I managed to understand the Germans only left an hour or so ago so they're probably still quite close. I hope to God they don't come back.'

'Bugger all we can do about it if they do, with only our revolvers. Look, there's some sort of cart and an ancient car just turned up and they expect us to get into them. These Resistance chappies won't be best pleased when they discover there aren't actually any British tanks arriving here.'

'Roger that, Skip.'

They were taken to Roye, a small French town, and introduced to the colonel of the Resistance who also happened to be the mayor. With a lot of hand-waving and schoolboy French eventually Alex managed to explain that they weren't in fact liberators but had landed because they'd run out of fuel. A dispatch rider on a motorbike left immediately to try and get through the German line and deliver the message.

The mayor explained that he would do his best to keep his men in line but that they wouldn't be happy when they discovered the truth of the situation.

They were returned to the airfield as it had been decided he and his blokes would sleep in the hangar. They removed their camp beds and sleeping bags and got themselves set up. Alex wasn't happy about any of it and just hoped the message had got through. They'd scarcely got settled when there was the sound of shots and bullets ricocheting around on the outside of the metal walls of the hangar.

The Maquis had arrived. They looked a dishevelled and dangerous bunch and had obviously come looking for trouble. To his surprise the scruffy buggers set up a couple of trestles and more black bread, cheese and wine was produced. He nodded to his men but it was with some reluctance that they joined in with the second undeserved welcome party.

The leader spoke a little English and together they managed to hold a reasonably coherent conversation. The French Resistance men were disappointed that there wasn't actually a breakthrough by the British Army and they were concerned that the Germans would see the Typhoons and come back to destroy them.

Alex understood that some Germans had already been rounded

up, forced to dig their own graves, and then been executed and put in them. Gruesome stuff. He refused point-blank to join in any such further expeditions, made it perfectly clear he was in command of the squadron and that the Allies would be arriving shortly. Any shooting of Germans in cold blood would be reported to the authorities.

He wasn't sure he could carry out this threat but it seemed to do the trick. They were left in peace but didn't sleep much and were roused early by the Resistance firing at the walls of the hangar again.

'Look at that, Skip, our kites sitting like seven ducks in a row. I can't believe the Germans didn't see them there,' Billy said.

They hung about for a few hours and then to their astonishment and relief, a group of British tanks, escorting a petrol bowser, appeared on the horizon. The major leading this advance party made the most of the situation.

Billy suggested that they flew in low formation over the town by way of thanks and he agreed. He led them up into the sky and then, with the sun behind them, they streaked in open formation across the airfield. They then circled and did the same across the town, much to the consternation but also the enjoyment of the populace.

11

Babs had started to write to Alex every week with snippets of news about the children, how they were growing and doing new things every day. He didn't reply as often, but his occasional letters were much appreciated.

Towards the end of August the entire family, plus Ned, were sitting in the garden enjoying a treat of scones with jam and delicious fresh cream whipped to a spreading consistency. Julia was sitting on a rug with her adoring older brother next to her.

'I don't suppose I should really give her half a scone,' Babs said as she handed one to her daughter. 'I'm sure someone told me babies her age shouldn't be eating anything but mashed food.'

'Charlie would have something to say if his little sister didn't get the same as him,' Grandma said. 'I must admit I expected him to be jealous of her but he's absolutely devoted. I think that's why Julia is so advanced.'

Ned and David were sprawled on the grass beside the little ones. Both of them were growing like weeds and she rather thought they would both be taller than Tom. She opened Alex's latest letter as she always read it to the family – just skipping over anything personal.

'Oh my word, just listen to this everyone: Alex's entire squadron got lost.' When she'd finished reading they were all laughing.

'Imagine that, Edward – what an exciting life that young man is leading. He's going to find it very dull when he comes back next year.'

'I should think that's exactly what they'll all be longing for, Elspeth. There's nothing wrong with dull after what they've been through.'

'Mummy, is my daddy lost again? I've not seen him for ages and ages.'

'No, sweetheart, he's not lost. He's very busy flying his aeroplane but he would much rather be home here with us.'

Ned scrambled up and came across to help himself to another scone and a second mug of tea. 'I'm really sorry that Mum's being so difficult. Alex wrote to her, you know, but it didn't make any difference. She's got it into her head that you and Tom are to blame for Jim's death. Dad's staying out of it but Valerie's sided with her. I don't reckon things will be sorted out until Alex is home.'

'It's a shame but it would be so much worse if she'd stopped you coming.'

Ned looked uncomfortable. 'She told me I couldn't come but I told her I was coming anyway and if she made a fuss I'd move in with you. She doesn't like it, but I don't care. I lost Jim. I'm not losing Tom and David and the rest of you as well.'

Grandpa had been listening to this conversation. 'Isn't that making things rather difficult for you?'

'Bloody horrible, but I'm not backing down. I don't work with Dad on the farm either and I've decided I don't want to take it on when Dad retires after all. I'm going to apply for Sandhurst – that's what Jim wanted to do so I'll do it for him.'

His bad language was ignored by her grandparents, which surprised her. They must think of him as old enough not to be reprimanded now.

David had joined them at the table. 'I'm going too, Babs. We're both going to become army medics.'

The thought of both boys being career soldiers filled her with dread but at least they wouldn't be fighting in this war.

'How does that work? Do the army pay for your medical training or do you have to do it before you sign up?'

'They pay for it and in return we have to stay for ten years. Seems a fair bargain to me. I thought you'd be upset, Babs.'

'You're both intelligent young men and quite capable of making up your own minds. Does that mean you'll be working as hospital porters like Tom in a couple of years?'

'Probably. When we're back at school we're going to talk to the master who runs the officer cadets. I should think he'll know the gen.'

David laughed. 'You wouldn't believe what Tom's been asked to do. He told me...'

'No, I really don't want to know. I told Tom to keep his gruesome stories to himself,' she replied with a smile. 'You're quite welcome to discuss anything medical with your grandfather but leave us out of it.'

The afternoon was brought to a premature end when the dogs chased two chickens and a duck across the children's rug, causing mayhem. The boys galloped off to catch Patch and Buttons. She dealt with an inconsolable baby who'd been terrified by the unexpected interruption. Charlie and Grandpa went in search of the birds and Grandma and Mrs B collected the scattered remains of the broken cups and plates.

'Come along, baby girl, I think you need a clean nappy. They were naughty doggies to chase the chickens like that, weren't they?'

* * *

That evening the boys retreated to their own domain. The children were asleep, and she sat with her grandparents in the sitting room with their nightly cocoa. She'd almost got used to not having sugar in it, but would be glad when rationing stopped, and the things they'd had to do without for so many years would be back on the menu.

'The dogs have never chased the chickens or ducks before. Did you find out why they did it today, Grandpa?'

'They were catching rats in the stables and those three unfortunate birds wandered in at just the wrong moment. I don't think it'll happen again. David and Ned have mended the hole in the fence and hopefully there'll be no more escapees ruining our afternoon tea.'

'Charlie will be old enough to start prep school at Brentwood next September. But I think he'd better go to the village school as I won't be able to get him there and back without a car.'

'Your father attended the village school until he was seven – it didn't do him any harm.'

'Edward, Babs, forgive me but I'm tired tonight. I'm going to retire.'

'I'll come with you, Elspeth. I'll bring the cocoa. Do you mind locking up for me, my dear girl?'

She loved this house but it was too big to run without extra help. They only used a third of the rooms at the moment, but once the war was over the rest of the house would be open again. Alex had never mentioned buying their own home, moving somewhere more manageable, and had promised Grandpa he would take over running the estate, managing the trust funds and so on, until her brothers were old enough to do it for themselves.

If both of them were intending to be doctors then she doubted either of them would want to live here permanently. David had his life planned out until he was in his late twenties; Tom would want to become a consultant and work in one of the big teaching hospitals in London.

The Grove would be redundant. Obviously, nothing would change whilst both her grandparents were alive but once they were gone – well, things would be different for all of them. It hardly seemed possible that last month there'd been a second wave of evacuations because of those horrible flying bombs. Those poor people must be at their wits' end, praying that the invasion forces moved rapidly and that Hitler surrendered.

* * *

When the invasion had begun back in June, Alex, like everyone else in the wing, had thought this bloody conflict would be finished before Christmas. Paris had been liberated last week but the Germans were fighting back in Belgium. God knows how many more people would have to die before Hitler surrendered.

The constant stream of both British and American bombers heading for German cities seemed excessive to him. Why bomb the civilians? Surely, they should be concentrating on destroying the German army, not killing bystanders?

Things were different now they were settled at Vitry. Sorties lasted longer and the flak continued to be heavy, indicating the Germans hadn't given up. He joined his squadron on their frequent trips to the town to enjoy what was on offer in the various bistros and bars.

On the 4th of September the Allies liberated Brussels. He went with three other blokes who'd borrowed a jeep and they drove the seventy miles to the city. The place was going wild celebrating being free from German occupation after so many years. Every available windowsill, wall and shopfront was draped not only with Belgian flags, but also Union Jacks.

'Blimey,' Billy said, 'where the hell have they been hiding these? We're the first pilots here. It'll be like this in London when the war's won and peace is declared.'

They were swept along by the crowd. Everyone wanted to buy them lunch and for the first time in many years Alex began to believe this nightmare really was coming to an end. That night they drove back full of delicious cheese, fresh bread, fancy pastries and wine.

He would have plenty to write about in his next letter to Babs. He never mentioned the losses, the fatigue, things that were part of being on the front line. The blokes were becoming battle-weary and he feared more mistakes would be made and lives would be lost through errors, rather than enemy action.

Two weeks after arriving at Vitry they were on the move again – this time to Deurne, an airfield just outside Antwerp. The more deadly V-2 rockets were now being fired at London. Bombs would destroy one launch pad and another would spring up further away.

His kite had suffered flak damage the last time up – nothing serious, but he was excluded from the next sortie. He would be back in business that afternoon.

There was a NAAFI wagon parked on the perimeter and he thought he would stroll over there and get himself a cup of cha and a wad. He stopped to talk to a stray dog that had adopted them.

'I'm going to get a bun. If you come with me, I'll give you a bit,' he said as he pulled the animal's floppy ears.

'I shouldn't get too close to that mutt, Alex. It's crawling with fleas,' a Canadian flyer called out from beside the van.

There was a faint whining noise and then an enormous explosion. The NAAFI van disintegrated. The last thing he remembered was being plastered with bits of cake and biscuits then a searing pain in his shoulder before everything went black.

* * *

He came round in the hospital ward. 'Good afternoon, Squadron Leader, back in the land of the living? Unfortunately, you were hit by a piece of flying shrapnel. I've taken it out, but I'm afraid you're out of action for the foreseeable. I'm not sure if you'll get full use of your arm again.'

Alex looked at the medic. 'Sod me! Almost killed by a flying NAAFI van. Were there many casualties?'

'Sadly, the two young ladies inside the wagon died, and those standing close have serious injuries from which they might or might not recover. You were one of the lucky ones. If you hadn't stopped to talk to that dog you might well have been killed.'

'Exactly what injury have I suffered?' He moved his hand and flexed his forearm and they seemed to work all right.

'The metal shattered your shoulder. We've patched it up as best we can, but it's highly likely movement will be severely restricted making it impossible for you to fly.'

'Not exactly the heroic end to my military career I'd hoped for. I'm sorry about the girls and the other blokes. I've got off lightly. What the hell was it that blew up the van?'

'A V-2 rocket misfired and came down here instead of heading for London.'

'How long am I going to be in here?'

'You'll be returning to jolly old Blighty tomorrow. Ah, the wing co is on his way to speak to you. Good luck, Alex. You've done your bit, just be glad you can go home relatively unscathed.'

There was no point in writing to Babs as he would be back in England before a letter could arrive. He was being transferred to a

London hospital where he would have to stay for a few days before probably being discharged. No, he might actually be demobbed – removed from duty altogether.

He wasn't sure how he felt about that. He'd expected to return when it was over, satisfied he'd done his bit for the war effort. His friends would still be fighting whilst he would be invalided out.

No one came to see him apart from his commanding officer. That's the way it was. The chaps welcomed you back when you were fit, raised a glass to you in the mess if you died, but otherwise they just got on with their job and forgot about you.

That night the disappointment at not being able to carry on flying gradually dissipated to be replaced by overwhelming relief that he was going home to be with his family. He blinked back unwanted tears at the thought that there would be one person missing. Jim had had so much potential and it had been snuffed out in such a stupid way.

* * *

After a lot of arguing on his part, instead of sending him to a London hospital they transferred him by ambulance to Brentwood. He didn't have good memories of this hospital as the last time he'd been there it had been when Babs had been so desperately ill after the birth.

A lot of men in white coats fussed over him when he arrived. He was prodded and poked, and for some reason no one was smiling. He had begun to feel unwell yesterday and being bounced around in an ambulance for a couple of hours hadn't helped.

Someone attached a tube to his arm, he was stabbed in the arse with a giant needle, and then allowed to sleep. If he'd only damaged his shoulder why was he feeling so rough?

He drifted in and out of consciousness for the next few hours – in fact felt pretty grim – and his shoulder throbbed painfully.

Whilst he was being given a quick blanket bath he asked one of the nurses if his family had been informed that he was at the hospital.

'I don't believe so, Squadron Leader Everton. As soon as I have finished here I'll ask Sister if I can ring your wife for you.'

'Will I be allowed visitors? Isn't there some rule about it?'

'As you're in a side ward, Squadron Leader, and in the circumstances, visitors will be allowed at any time they wish to come.'

He was puzzled as to what circumstances she could be referring to and decided he might be the only serviceman back from the front and therefore had special privileges. She returned and fussed about checking his pulse and his temperature and, after stabbing him in the arse again, she gave him the good news.

'Squadron Leader Everton, your wife is on her way to see you.'

'That's splendid. Thank you for doing that.'

He drifted off to sleep. When he woke it was to find his darling girl sitting at his side holding his hand. She wasn't looking at him, wasn't aware that he was conscious and it gave him a moment or two to focus his thoughts. Why was she looking so sad? Her face was pale, dark smudges under her eyes, when he'd expected to see her bubbling over with happiness that he was home in one piece.

* * *

The strident tones of the telephone summoned Babs from the sitting room where she'd been sitting with her grandparents watching Charlie playing with Julia on the rug.

'The Grove, Mrs Everton speaking.'

'Mrs Everton, this is Staff Nurse Edwards at Brentwood Hospital. Your husband arrived here yesterday morning. He has a serious shoulder injury that has become infected and is considered critical but stable. Because of his condition you can visit at any time you wish.'

'What happened? How is he in Brentwood? I thought he was in Belgium somewhere.'

'He insisted on being transferred here from London. The consultant will speak to you when you arrive, Mrs Everton.'

'What ward is he on?'

'If you report to reception then they will direct you.'

Babs had difficulty replacing the telephone receiver on its stand as her hands were shaking so much. Alex was home but he was – what had she said? 'Critical but stable.' What did that mean? She raced to the sitting room.

'Grandpa, Alex is in hospital in Brentwood. The nurse said I can go and see him any time. He's critical but stable. What exactly does that mean in medical terms?'

'It means, my dear girl, that he is not dead. That he's seriously injured, but he's fighting back.' There was the sound of David and Tom dropping their bicycles outside the back door. 'Excellent, now your brothers are home they can take care of the children. I'll give that rogue Peterson a ring – he's usually got some petrol in his van.'

She quickly explained the urgency to the boys. They flew upstairs and changed out of their uniforms and were back to take charge of the children. Grandma was resting. Everyone was very protective of her although Babs couldn't see much difference and was hopeful that the diagnosis of dementia was incorrect.

'Charlie, Grandpa and I have got to go to Brentwood. Uncle Tom and Uncle David are going to look after you, along with Mrs B and Grandma. We might not be back before you go to bed so I'll explain everything to you tomorrow morning. Be a good boy.'

'I'll look after Julia for you, Mummy. I'm four now. I'm not a little boy any more.'

She leant down and hugged him and then kissed the top of the baby's head. Julia was busy knocking down the towers of bricks that her brother was building for her and not interested in anything else.

Half an hour later Mr Peterson was driving them to Brentwood in his van. He was a jobbing builder and therefore had access to petrol as his work was considered essential. She wasn't quite sure why her grandpa considered the man to be a rogue. As far as she was concerned, he was a pleasant sort of person – a bit rough around the edges, but nothing worse than that.

Being squashed in the front seat, half on, half off Grandpa's lap, wasn't an enjoyable experience but a lot better than having to cycle on her own. It was impossible to hold a conversation over the noise so she sat, trying to brace herself against the side of the van, and prayed that Alex wasn't as ill as she feared.

The rattletrap rocked to a halt outside the hospital. 'Give us a bell, Doc, if you want a lift home.'

'Thank you, Mr Peterson, your help was much appreciated but I'm not sure when either of us will be able to return.'

Babs was already halfway up the steps and heading for the reception desk. Just the smell of the place brought back horrible memories of being rushed in here several months ago. Was this going to be the place where she actually lost him?

Grandpa looked at her and then took charge. He had worked here on and off for years and the receptionist recognised him. He knew exactly where to take her and kept his arm firmly around her shoulders.

'Chin up, my dear girl. Alex has everything to live for. He is here. He's got a fighting chance and when he gets through this, he'll be home for good.'

'I don't even know why he's here or what happened. If I go into him, will you find the consultant? He's bound to tell you the truth.'

They were now outside the open door of a small side room. She froze in the doorway. She scarcely recognised her husband as the man lying, deathly pale, in the bed. When he'd finally got home after months as an evader and being in a Spanish concentration camp, he'd been thin but hadn't looked as bad as this.

There was a nurse checking his pulse and temperature. 'Mrs Everton, you'll be pleased to know that his temperature has gone down a little. He is still considered critical but his condition is improving slightly.'

Babs slumped on the hard, wooden chair beside the bed and reached out and took his hand. He'd obviously been injured in his shoulder as she could see the bandages and his pyjama sleeve on his right side was empty. For a horrible moment she'd thought he'd lost his arm but then saw it was lying across his stomach inside his pyjamas.

She leant over and kissed his forehead. It was hot and dry. Was this caused by an infection in his wound? His pulse was rapid, his breathing shallow. Why had they moved him from London when he was so ill? This must have made him worse.

Whilst he slept she had time to study his features more closely. There was engine oil ingrained in lines on his face that hadn't been there before. He looked utterly exhausted.

Her eyes filled and surreptitiously she withdrew her handkerchief from her pocket and wiped them. She was going to put a brave face on and pretend that she wasn't terrified she was going to lose him for good this time.

12

Alex still felt bloody awful but marginally better than he had before. Babs raised her head and her smile was everything he'd hoped it would be.

'Darling, I'm back and this time to stay. Ignore whatever the medics tell you – I'm not going to kick the bucket. I've got too much to live for.'

She bent down and kissed him – not on the mouth but on his forehead. 'Although you look dreadful, you do look a bit better than you did a couple of hours ago. Grandpa spoke to your consultant and it seems your wound is infected and they're giving you something called penicillin. It's supposed to be a wonder drug and only available to service people.'

He managed a weak grin. 'That must be what they're injecting me with. I'll have a backside like a pincushion by the time I'm better.'

She returned his smile. Just seeing his beloved girl was enough for the moment. There had been moments, several of them, when he thought he wouldn't make it.

'Don't try and talk, Alex – I can see it's hard for you. I'll tell you all about our wonderful children and you can fall asleep if you want to. I won't be offended.'

'I'm knackered – we all are – so don't be surprised if I sleep for the next few days. I've got a lot of catching up to do.'

Edward swam into his line of vision. Things were still rather blurry. 'The more you sleep the quicker you'll recover, my boy. The penicillin is working and if it continues to do so you will be out of the woods by tomorrow and hopefully home within a week or two.'

Alex squeezed his wife's hand and then let sleep overtake him. He was vaguely aware of being messed about with by nurses, of his shoulder being examined, but mostly he just stayed asleep.

'Alex, I know you're tired but you've got to wake up and have something to eat and drink. You won't get better until you do.'

He opened his eyes. The blackouts were drawn and the lights were on. It must be late. 'Babs, what are you doing here? There's no need for you to sit next to me. Go home and come back tomorrow – I'm not going to die in the night so don't look so worried.'

'The doctor who just came round said he will take you off the critical list if you eat something. Grandpa is an absolute trouper. He persuaded someone to drive him home and Mrs B has sent us both in a delicious supper. And I'm not going anywhere. I'm spending the night here.'

Moving was painful and difficult but he managed to shuffle himself more or less upright. He hadn't noticed the nurse lurking in the background but immediately she pushed some pillows behind him.

'That's the ticket, Squadron Leader – you look ever so much better. I'm going to fetch you both a nice cup of tea to go with your supper.'

Whatever he ate, it was delicious. He thought it was some sort of pasty filled with chicken and ham. He munched his way through two of these and then washed them down with two cups of tea. How could doing something so simple have exhausted him?

'You should be home with the children, not camping out here, darling.'

'They've given me a pillow and a blanket and I'll be absolutely splendid. I'll pack away what's left of this and we can have it if you wake up later. There are scones and jam and some fruit. I'm going to find the loo. I'll be back soon.'

Fortunately, a student nurse came in to take his temperature and so on and provided him with a receptacle in the nick of time.

'Still up a little, but nothing to worry about. Sister said that you'll be moved on to the main ward tomorrow. You're off the danger list.'

'I certainly feel a lot better. I need a few days' kip and I'll be ready to be discharged. My father-in-law's a medical man – he can take care of my injury.'

'Good heavens, you won't be leaving here for another two weeks at least. I'll be back in four hours for your next injection.'

She whisked away and he couldn't keep his eyes open. Vaguely he was aware that Babs had climbed onto the bed and was snuggling up against him. He sighed. It was worth getting shot up by an exploding NAAFI van just to be here with her.

The night sister arrived with his penicillin but instead of making a fuss, waking Babs up, she patted him on the shoulder and left things as they were.

The bed was empty when he next opened his eyes. The curtains were back and the blackouts up so it must be morning. He was starving and needed a pee. Desperately. There was no bell to ring and he didn't want to yell.

Thank God! There was a china container like the one he'd used before on the windowsill. All he needed to do was get out of bed, walk a few steps and get it. There was a strong possibility his legs would give way but the alternative was far worse for his dignity and comfort.

Slowly he sat up, and then swivelled and put his legs on the lino. So far so good. He couldn't use his right hand to push himself upwards so would have to rely on his left. Pity he was right-handed. If he left it any longer he might as well stay where he was and pee on the floor.

He stood up, staggered across the small room, snatched up the necessary item and tottered back to the bed. Babs walked in mid flow. She promptly turned round and disappeared.

'I'll fetch the nurse. There are some things I'm just not prepared to do. It's quite enough dealing with Julia's nappies.'

Her laughter was genuine and he joined in. He didn't blame her. When he got home he would sleep in a different room until he was fully fit. Despite the fact that she'd slept beside him last night it didn't necessarily mean she'd changed her mind about making love.

An hour later a porter came to wheel his bed into the main ward. 'I've got to go now, darling, but I'll come...'

'No, don't visit again. I'll be home in a few days. Ignore whatever the consultant says, I'm going to discharge myself when I finish this course of injections.'

'I'll speak to Grandpa. If he's happy for you to come home then we'll arrange for someone to come and get you. Promise me you won't just walk out of here.'

'Scout's honour. It makes sense, sweetheart. I'll get better quicker with my family around me and it'll be so much easier for you.'

The porter was getting impatient. 'Behave yourself, Alex. I'll tell the children that their daddy will be home very soon.'

* * *

At The Grove nobody listened to the nine o'clock news any more. Now Alex was out of danger it no longer seemed important. Everybody knew the war was won; it was just a matter of when.

There'd been more than enough of gloom and despair over the past five years. As far as Babs was concerned it was over now that Alex was back and was being invalided out of the RAF. He'd been a career pilot – not a volunteer – but she didn't think he'd mind very much having both feet back on the ground whilst the war was on. He had intended to remain in the RAF when the war finished or maybe become a commercial pilot but now that was no longer possible.

Grandpa had spoken to the consultant and in three days' time her husband would be brought home in an ambulance. The district nurse was going to call to change his dressing and the local doctor had agreed to keep an eye on him too.

'Grandma, I think it would be better if Alex has my room and I move. I can quite easily go to the nearest bathroom if I need to in the night but he can't. He needs to be close to the facilities.'

'That seems like a sensible suggestion, my dear, as, no doubt, you will wish to rejoin him as soon as he is well.'

'We've got the rest of our lives ahead of us. Things are going to be different, and it's going to take a bit of adjustment. Remember, we've never lived like a normal family as Alex was rarely home.'

'When you first married and lived near Hornchurch surely you were together then?'

'We were, but he was on the base more than he was with me. Anyway, I was pregnant and that won't happen again, will it?'

'No, Babs, but you've got two beautiful children, a boy and a girl, which in my opinion is more than enough.'

'Do you think he's going to be bored stuck here with just us after having so much excitement? I know initially he'll be happy to potter about whilst he recuperates. What about afterwards? He no longer has a career. He will soon come to resent living on my money if he doesn't.'

'He has his Higher School Certificate so I see no reason why he shouldn't go to university. Edward was telling me the government's making places available at colleges and universities especially for returning servicemen. He won't be the only one in that position, my dear.'

'I've no idea what he might want to study; the subject's never come up. I can't see him becoming a stockbroker, accountant or a banker, can you?'

'What about the law? I could see him as a barrister – he would be very dashing in robes and a wig.'

'Yes, that might be suitable. However, he would have to attend a London university and then do years of further study whilst attached to a law firm – again in the city. Commuting from here would be really difficult so I expect he'd have to find digs and come home at weekends.'

Instead of being horrified at the thought of not having Alex with her during the week she realised she would actually prefer not to have him around all the time. She loved him, no doubt about that, but she would get on with him better if he wasn't under her feet all day.

Tom helped her sort the new sleeping arrangements. It was strange but the age difference, just over eight years, seemed to be shrinking. Her brother was now practically an adult and no longer needed her guidance. He was more of a friend than anything else.

'You should do something to celebrate having Alex home for good, Babs.'

'I only hope you won't have to leave instead. I heard Grandpa saying there's likely to be conscription, national service of some sort, for several years after the end of this conflict.'

'I know. We've talked about it at school. As long as I'm in full-time education I'll be exempt – and that will be for six years. I don't think a qualified doctor will be asked to do any sort of compulsory service, do you?'

'You're probably right. Sit down for a minute. There's something important I need to talk to you about. I suppose we should also include David, but you can tell him later. He and Ned are riding at the moment.'

'What's up, Sis? You've not been yourself these past few days but I thought it was just worrying about Alex.'

'It is partly about Alex, but not about his health. We both thought he would continue as a pilot. We've never discussed what he would do if he couldn't fly. Did he say anything to Jim that he might have shared with you about what he would do if he left the RAF?'

'I know what he doesn't want to do and that's be a farmer. I shouldn't worry about it; he'll have some plans of his own worked out by the time he gets home at the end of the week. What else did you want to talk about?'

She smiled ruefully. Nothing was a problem when you were young. 'It's this house and the estate. It's far too big for us and I can't see either you or David wanting to live here permanently. Obviously, nothing will change whilst our grandparents are still around, but after that, if you and David want to sell it I'd have no objection.'

He looked at her in astonishment. 'Bloody hell! I didn't know you weren't inheriting. We're not real Sinclairs – it shouldn't come to us at all.'

'I thought you both knew that Grandpa changed his will. I've got my massive trust fund – I don't need anything else. The Grove will give you and David an excellent start in life.'

He was quiet for a few minutes, sat with his eyes half closed, tapping his fingers on his knee. 'Okay. I agree with you. Keep things as they are and then sell. Hopefully, it's not something any of us will have to consider for years.'

'I'm glad we've got that settled but I wish I hadn't blurted out the information. Please don't tell David. I'm sure Grandpa wants to tell you himself when he thinks you're old enough to understand why he's done it. Also, you are a real Sinclair. It's on your birth certificate, identity card and so on.'

They finished making the bed and she looked around to see that everything was ready for Alex, that his civilian clothes were in the closet and everything she needed had now been moved.

Tom was about to go but then changed his mind and reached into his pocket and handed her a letter. 'I got this from John this morning. You'd better read it. I think the poor bloke's unhinged.'

Her heart thudded uncomfortably. She could think of only one reason why John would write to Tom. Was her guilty secret now about to be revealed?

* * *

Alex didn't have to discharge himself; the consultant agreed he was fit enough to continue his recuperation at home. Therefore, less than a week after his arrival at Brentwood he was in the back of an ambulance being transported to Ingatestone.

They were travelling at speed as the vehicle was on an emergency call and was going to drop him off on the way past. Every bump in the road jarred his shoulder but the discomfort was worth it as in a few minutes he would see his daughter. She'd been a few months old when he'd last seen her on that horrible visit just after Jim had died. Now she was over six months old. He would be a stranger to her, possibly to Charlie also.

He swallowed a lump in his throat as he recalled how his son had reacted when he'd returned after being away for six months. Hopefully, things would be different this time.

The ambulance screeched to a halt at the end of the drive. One of the men ran round and opened the rear door and he scrambled out. They didn't stop to see if he was capable of making his way to the house – the door was slammed and the vehicle roared off to collect someone in the village who'd had a heart attack.

The weather was perfect: warm autumn sunshine, the trees just beginning to turn from green to gold and everything was right in his world – well, as right as it could be in the circumstances. He'd scarcely walked a hundred yards when the dogs streaked down the drive to greet him.

His right arm was in a sling so he fussed each in turn with his left hand. He was getting more adept at using this and thought he wouldn't need much help in the dressing department. Then Charlie appeared running flat out, closely followed by Babs with the baby in her arms.

Running was out of the question at the moment, but he increased his pace and reached down and scooped up his son when he arrived at his knees. 'Charlie, you've grown so much since I last saw you. I left a little boy and now I've got a big boy.'

'Daddy, Daddy, you've come home to us at last. Does your arm hurt? Can you play cricket with me? Here comes my mummy with my sister.'

'I'll have to put you down, sweetheart, so I can give them a hug. I've only got one arm that works at the moment.'

His eyes weren't on Babs but on Julia who was screeching with laughter from being bounced about. His daughter was even more beautiful than he'd remembered. Her hair was long enough to thread a ribbon through and the colour of autumn leaves – just like his.

He held out his arm and Babs handed the baby to him. 'Hello, little one. You don't know me but I'm your daddy.'

She chuckled and reached up to pat his face and pull his hair. Her eyes had changed colour and were no longer blue but green like her mother's. He was mesmerised and for a moment forgot there was anyone else he should be greeting.

'Hello, Alex, you look remarkably well for a man who was on his deathbed a week ago.'

He looked up and smiled sheepishly. 'Sorry, darling, I was blown over by our beautiful girl. She has my hair and looks like me but she's got your eyes.'

Charlie overheard this and tugged at his uniform jacket. 'Daddy, why don't I have your hair? I don't look like you. I want to have red hair like you and Julia.'

Alex hastily handed the baby over and then picked his son up. 'You look like your mummy and like your uncles. Your Aunt Valerie has hair like mine and two children – they are your cousins. They haven't got red hair either. It's just how things are.'

The little boy hugged him and covered his cheeks with sloppy kisses. 'I love you, Daddy. Don't ever go away again – promise me that.'

'I might have to go away for a few days at a time but never for months. I can certainly promise that.'

Babs was very quiet. Something was wrong with her but this wasn't the time or the place to ask. Tom and David suddenly appeared from the front of the house and ran towards him.

If his wife's greeting had been subdued, then the two boys made up for it. Edward, Elspeth and Mrs B were equally effusive. A celebration lunch had been prepared and he had no opportunity to speak to Babs in private until later that night.

'Shall we go for a walk in the garden, Babs? The boys can listen out for the children for half an hour.'

13

Babs almost refused to go with Alex. She didn't want to ruin his homecoming by showing him the letter John had written to Tom.

She didn't want to hold his hand so walked ahead of him. From his expression he was hurt by her rejection but he would understand when he read the letter.

There was still a rose garden although the lawn had been turned over to vegetable growing. The marble bench was the perfect place to sit in the evening sunshine. It might be the third week in September but the weather was still pleasantly warm.

'I'm sorry if I seem distracted. I've not been able to sleep or think clearly since Tom gave me this yesterday. Here, read it for yourself.'

He made no comment, just pulled the letter from the envelope and began to read. She knew it off by heart having read it so often.

Dear Tom,

I have something important to tell you that I think you deserve to know. It's not information I care to put in a letter so I intend to come to Essex at the end of the month so I can speak to you and David in person.

I am persona non grata with both Barbara and Alex so cannot come to The Grove and will meet you outside your school in Brentwood on Friday twenty-ninth of September.

I look forward to seeing you both again soon,

John

'Babs, this is not good. What did you say to Tom?'

'I just said that John's not the man he used to be and that Tom doesn't have to meet him if he doesn't want to.'

'Didn't he ask if you knew what this information was?'

'Strangely, he didn't ask. This is an absolute nightmare. I don't want my brothers to think that I'm... that I'm a slut to have slept with two men within the space of two weeks.'

'Christ, is that all you're worried about? Your precious reputation? Think of the damage it would do to Charlie, if you don't care how it's going to affect me.'

She stared at him in shock. John wasn't the only one who'd changed. The old Alex would never have spoken to her so unkindly.

'You've only been back a few hours and already you're being absolutely vile. I'm going to bed. You can do what you like as long as it's nowhere near me.'

She stormed off expecting him to come after her but he didn't. She bitterly regretted her outburst. She'd been stewing about this letter, and the consequences that would follow John's revelation, and had expected Alex to be sympathetic. Instead, he had turned on her – accused her of being selfish.

Anyone would have mentioned what concerned themselves before going on to how it affected others and it didn't make her selfish, it made her normal. All he'd had to do was reassure her and then they could have gone on to discuss the implications for everyone else.

She'd cried more than enough over the past few months and wasn't going to give in to tears tonight. The plan that her grandparents had come up with in this eventuality would prevent John from making any legal challenges, from trying to get visitation rights to Charlie. However, all those that mattered to her would know that his accusations were true.

Mrs B had been there when John had stayed at the house; she would remember what he looked like and only have to look at Charlie to understand the truth. Her brothers would be devastated that she'd kept this from them. They liked John, but they adored Alex and this would complicate matters.

Alex could no longer say that he was Charlie's actual father without feeling awkward in front of the family. It was quite possible he would then favour his daughter, which would make things even harder for her son – no, their son.

After checking on the children she went to bed foregoing her usual cocoa. An hour later she heard Alex come up and stiffened, expecting him to knock on the door, but he went straight into his room. Would it ever be *their* room again?

She was always up first because Julia woke around six. Charlie usually appeared an hour or so later, which gave her precious time alone with her daughter.

This morning when she went in to the nursery the cot was empty. For a second she was paralysed with fear, then realised that Alex had got there first. The house was silent. Why couldn't she hear them in the kitchen? Julia always had her morning bottle first thing and then waited to have breakfast with everyone else.

The back door was wide open. Alex had obviously taken the baby and the dogs into the garden. She often did this herself so didn't blame him for wanting to familiarise himself with the place that was going to be his home now. For the past five years he'd been moved from place to place, often living in the most primitive conditions, so he must be revelling in the luxury of being back at The Grove.

Then she remembered he only had one good arm and was worried that he might drop Julia who constantly wriggled when she was being carried.

'Alex, where are you?' There was no answer; her shout was loud enough to disturb the pigeons in the trees along the edge of what used to be the lawn. She didn't want to wake anyone else up by shouting a second time. Either he wasn't out here or he was ignoring her. Neither possibility pleased her.

The dogs were with him and they would have heard her if they were in earshot. She'd been outside too long. If Charlie got up and went to look for her he could get into all sorts of mischief. Alex should have told her that he intended to wander off with the baby. As far as their daughter was concerned, he was a stranger.

She paused in the kitchen long enough to put the kettle on and then listened at the bottom of the stairs. All quiet – if Charlie was awake she would hear him calling or banging about. There was something missing in the boot room – what was it?

The pram had gone. Alex had taken Julia out in that and she could think of only one place he might have gone. He was taking the baby to Home Farm. He had no right to do this without her permission. Had he already decided that John was going to claim Charlie so there was little point in taking their son to visit his parents? There couldn't be any other explanation for why he'd sneaked off so early in the morning. No doubt he'd hoped to be back before she got up. Work started on a farm at daybreak so there was no danger of finding the house asleep when he got there.

She hadn't spoken to her mother-in-law for weeks and although she was desperate to know if Alex was actually there with Julia, she couldn't face the frosty reception she would get when Mrs Everton picked up the phone.

* * *

Alex decided to walk to the village. Everything would be closed and there was so little traffic on the road there was no danger of the dogs getting run over. He remembered pushing Charlie in the same pram but it had been much easier to manoeuvre it when he'd had both arms fully functioning.

Negotiating the drive was no problem as it was in good repair but he couldn't say the same about the pavement. The baby gurgled and babbled, waved her little chubby hands around and beamed at him. 'I'm your daddy, sweetheart, and I can't believe I'm going to be here to watch you grow up. I missed so much of your brother's first years.' Talking to his daughter as if she was an adult was hardly sensible but Julia didn't mind and laughed and clapped every time they hit a bump in the path.

The dogs abandoned him after half a mile and he didn't call them back. They were as familiar with the area as he was and wouldn't get lost. He reached the churchyard and pushed the pram through the gate. His ancestors were buried here but his brother couldn't join them.

His throat tightened. To not have Jim's body to bury would have made losing him so much worse for his parents. Julia had flopped back against the lace-edged pillow and fallen asleep. Pushing the pram over the bumpy grass was impossible one-handed and she would probably wake up. The churchyard was deserted. It would be perfectly safe to leave her sleeping whilst he went to pay his respects to his grandparents who were buried at the far side of the churchyard.

Gently he covered her with the blanket, checked her harness

was secure, put the brake on, and looked at his watch. He wouldn't be gone more than ten minutes and his precious daughter was sound asleep and wouldn't even know.

He'd deliberately parked the pram where he could see it until he stepped off the path. This meant the baby would only be out of sight for a few minutes. He glanced round for a final time at the sleeping infant and then turned left and made his way through the tombstones to the area at the back of the churchyard that belonged to his family.

His shoulder was aching unpleasantly, he felt light-headed and thought he should have eaten something before he set off. His eyes widened when he saw a fresh headstone. He increased his pace and dropped to his knees beside it.

James Michael Everton
1928–1944
Gone Too Soon

There was no freshly dug mound of earth, no flowers, just the grey marble headstone to mark Jim's passing. He buried his head in his hands and cried for the first time since his brother had died so tragically.

He couldn't stay here – Julia had been out of sight for too long already. He scrambled to his feet, his head spun and his legs buckled. He fought to stay conscious but the blackness overwhelmed him.

* * *

Charlie woke up early and wanted to know where his sister was. 'Where's Julia, Mummy?'

'Daddy has taken her for a walk in the pram. He's gone to see Nanna Everton.'

'I want to see my Nanna Everton. Why didn't he take me too? Is it because I don't have red hair like Julia?'

'It's got nothing to do with the colour of your hair, darling; it's just that your daddy got up early and so did your sister. I'm sure he'll take you both next time.'

Mrs B was busy getting breakfast for all of them. When her son Joe had worked outside and lived upstairs, she and Joe had eaten separately. Mrs B was now considered a member of the family and they all ate together in the kitchen. Despite the closeness and informality, the housekeeper still refused to call anyone by their Christian names.

'Good morning, Mrs Everton. The little one's sleeping late today.'

'Good morning, Mrs B. Alex has taken Julia to see his parents. I'm not sure if they'll be back for breakfast.'

'About time things were sorted out. Come along, little man, it's boiled eggs and soldiers today. I'll get yours ready first.'

Babs kept glancing at the clock on the French dresser, becoming more anxious as the minutes ticked by. Her grandparents arrived and she beckoned them into the sitting room before explaining the problem.

'I'm very cross with Alex. He shouldn't have taken Julia to Home Farm without speaking to me first. He's been gone for three hours. I'm getting worried but don't like to telephone myself.'

'I'll do it, my dear girl,' said Grandpa. 'Most inconsiderate of Alex to be away so long. Also, remarkably stupid considering he was critically ill just over a week ago.'

How could she have forgotten that Alex should really still be in hospital? Instead of being cross with him she should have gone out to look for him in case something had happened.

Grandpa returned looking grim. 'He's not been there. Get the boys up. The three of you need to go in search of him. I'm not fit enough to rush about the countryside but I'll be ready with my medical bag if needed.'

Her brothers dressed and were downstairs by the time she'd packed what she needed for the baby.

'I'll cycle to the farm,' David said. 'What do I do if I find him passed out and the baby screaming?'

'Pedal back here. I'll be waiting,' Grandpa told him.

'I'll go towards the village, Babs. I've got enough coppers to make a phone call if I find him.'

'Thank you, Tom. I'll get Silver harnessed to the cart. If he's not well we'll need something to bring him back in.'

Charlie was oblivious to the excitement. Grandma was keeping him amused and he'd be perfectly happy whilst they were out. Her mare went as well in harness as she did under saddle, which was fortunate.

'I'll come with you, my dear girl. I can sit beside you and still leave plenty of room for Alex on the rear seat.'

'I hoped you'd decide to come with me, Grandpa. I've got a very bad feeling about this. I should have rung when I discovered Alex was missing. Why hasn't someone found them? It's after ten now. The shops in the village will be open – if he'd gone there somebody must have seen him.'

She urged Silver into a trot and they'd covered half the distance when David caught them up. 'No sign of them my way. I'll go ahead and help Tom.'

He'd barely been gone five minutes when he reappeared pedalling furiously with his head down. He skidded to a halt beside them, making the mare shy. 'He's in the churchyard. He's a bit groggy, but Tom's helping him.' Her brother's face was white and he couldn't continue.

'David, what about Julia?'

'She isn't there. Someone must have taken her whilst Alex was passed out.' He didn't wait for her reaction but spun his bike around and raced off.

'Taken? Kidnapped?'

'No, don't look so stricken, my dear girl. I'm sure a passer-by heard her crying and has taken her somewhere safe.'

She slapped the reins on Silver's neck and urged her into a canter. Her heart was pounding. Not with fear that Alex was very unwell but that Grandpa was wrong and her beautiful baby had actually been abducted.

The cart rattled and bumped into the village. She reined in hard outside the churchyard. 'I'm going to look for her. You can look after Alex.'

She gave him no time to argue. She jumped from the cart and ran to the village shop. She burst in, slamming the door back, and the queue of ladies waiting to be served looked round in shock.

'My baby was taken from the churchyard in her pram. Does anybody know where she is?'

Immediately she was surrounded by fussing and tutting but nobody knew anything about it. One lady, still in her wrap-around apron, offered to organise a search.

'Thank you. I'm going to all the shops. My husband had taken her for a walk. He's just out of hospital and collapsed. Julia was taken whilst he was unconscious.'

'How absolutely dreadful, Mrs Everton. I can't imagine that anyone would do such a thing,' the vicar's wife said sympathetically.

'Doctor Sinclair is taking care of my husband. I've got to find my baby.'

She dashed out as abruptly as she'd arrived and stood for a few seconds on the pavement looking up and down the High Street, hoping she might see somebody pushing the old pram towards her.

Ingatestone was a small village. Everybody knew everyone else, so why didn't somebody in the post office know where Julia was?

There were several lanes that meandered from the main thoroughfare and all had a scattering of cottages and houses on either side. She was hesitating, not sure where to look next, when she saw two children peering around the side of the cottage a short distance away.

She called out to them but they vanished. Was it possible children had taken Julia and were now afraid to bring her back in case they got into trouble?

Her heart slowed, the sick feeling in her stomach lessened. Her baby was safe. Children wouldn't hurt her. The ladies emerged from the shop behind her, their shopping forgotten.

'I think some children might have taken her. Do you know what family lives down that turning?'

The vicar's wife replied. 'The Smiths – they've got half a dozen children but sadly the latest addition to the family was stillborn. Quickly, I'll take you there. It makes sense that they might have thought taking back a baby for their mother would make her feel better.'

There was no need to go down the lane as a dishevelled lady, her hair still in curlers and her slippers on, appeared pushing the missing pram.

Babs broke into a run and reached her side in seconds. Julia was fast asleep, none the worse her adventure.

'They never meant no 'arm, ma'am. Me nippers was just trying to help. I changed her bum, gave her somefink to eat and she's right as ninepence. Sorry to 'ave upset you like.'

The children were snivelling, looking terrified. She crouched down beside them. 'Thank you so much for taking care of my baby.

Her daddy wasn't well. He only came out of hospital last week and shouldn't have been walking about on his own.'

Whilst she'd been talking she'd been rummaging in her pockets and come up with a handful of silver and coppers. There was probably just over a pound – that would do. 'Here you are, this is your reward for finding Julia.' She tipped the coins into their outstretched hands and their faces lit up.

David arrived on his bicycle. 'You found her, thank God. Alex is beside himself. We've got him into the cart and Grandpa is taking him home. I need to go with them as he isn't able to walk without Tom and I holding him up.'

'It's only a mile and a half. Don't wait for us – I'll walk back with Julia.'

'Good show. See you later.'

Babs thanked everybody who'd shown such concern for her missing child and then turned the pram around and began the trek home. She had plenty of time to think about what had happened and her part in it. Only now did the possible gravity of the situation become apparent.

Alex should never have gone out. He should have known better – after all, hadn't he been discharged on the understanding that he would rest for the next two weeks? What had possessed him to walk all the way to the village?

14

Alex hadn't the strength to make his own way to bed and it took the combined efforts of both boys to manoeuvre him up the narrow staircase.

Edward followed close behind with his medical bag. 'Put him on the bed, boys. I'll take it from here. Ask Mrs B to get a tray ready and then bring it up to me.'

'Babs must be furious with me. I shouldn't have gone out but I felt okay when I got up.'

'For an intelligent man you behaved remarkably stupidly. Good God, you could have died, Julia could have been injured and it would have been entirely your fault.'

Alex was too tired to argue. He raised his good arm in surrender and closed his eyes. He was barely aware of Edward fiddling about but was forced to pay attention when Babs came in carrying the baby.

'How are you feeling? I'm very cross with you, but you're far too unwell to be shouted out so I've decided to let it go.'

She sat on the edge of the bed with the baby on her lap. Even turning his head was an effort. 'Good show. I don't deserve to be forgiven. Won't happen again...' Everything was becoming fuzzy around the edges again.

'Don't go back to sleep, Alex. Your breakfast is here and I'm going to make sure that you eat it.'

He managed to drink the tea but chewing was impossible. He was relieved when the room was empty and he could sleep. Edward had reassured him that he wouldn't send him back to hospital unless his condition deteriorated.

* * *

He wasn't sure how long it was before he recovered sufficiently to sit up and take an interest in the world. He opened his eyes to see Charlie sitting on the end of the bed staring at him.

'Hello, son, does your mummy know that you're here?'

'She thinks I'm having a nap. Can I have my nap with you, Daddy?'

'There's plenty of room as long as you don't wriggle and hurt my bad shoulder. Do you know what day it is today?'

'It's a rainy day. I don't like rain as I can't go out and play.'

'Before you lie down with me you've got to tell Mummy. I don't want her worrying if she looks in your room and you're not there.'

The little boy rolled off the bed and ran to the door. Alex had expected him to go in search of Babs but instead he yelled at the top of his voice. Moments later she arrived outside the door.

'What are you doing out here, young man? I thought you were having a nap.'

'I am, Mummy, but I'm going to have it with my daddy because he's all on his own in there.'

She appeared in the doorway and her smile made him feel glad to be alive. 'Grandpa said that you just needed to sleep. After so many months, years really, of being sleep-deprived your body simply wanted to catch up. I'm so glad you're awake and looking almost well.'

'I'm starving and I need a pee.'

'I can fetch you some food but I'm not assisting with the other. There's a chamber pot under the bed. I'll go as far as handing it to you but the rest you'll have to do yourself.'

He grinned. 'Fair enough, but make it speedy, sweetheart, or there'll be a nasty accident.'

Before either of them could prevent it, Charlie dived head first under the bed and emerged clutching the empty pot triumphantly. 'Here you are, Daddy, I found it for you.'

'Thank you, sweetheart. Now go with your mummy and find me something to eat and drink. Then we can have a nap together.'

* * *

Edward gave him permission to totter to the bathroom that evening. 'You gave us a bit of scare, young man, but if you behave sensibly in future you're going to make a full and speedy recovery.'

'What's the date? I've lost track of time.'

'The twenty-eighth – Thursday. You were more or less comatose for three and a half days. I don't want you downstairs until next week but you can get out of bed tomorrow and sit in the chair by the window.'

'Righto. I won't be so stupid as to overdo it a second time. It's been good to see Ned but I wish things were smoothed over with my parents and sister.'

'Grief is a strange thing, Alex, and it affects different people in different ways. Give them time.'

Babs had promised to bring him a late-night snack when she came up. He was eating twice as much as he usually did and again Edward said this was to be expected. There was something about the date that bothered him but he couldn't remember what it was.

There was the welcome sound of a tray arriving and he was sitting up eager for his supper when she walked in. 'Babs, why am I worried about the date? My brain's still not fully functioning and I can't remember.'

'The boys are supposed to be meeting John tomorrow after school.' She put the tray on his lap and then sat on the end of the bed. 'I don't know if we should tell them before they go to school tomorrow. Then they don't have to meet him at all.'

His appetite deserted him and he pushed the tray onto the empty side of the bed. 'I'd forgotten about that. It doesn't make any difference to me if everybody knows I'm not his biological father. I'm just concerned about how he's going to feel. He could be traumatised for life.'

'That's not exactly helpful, Alex. I'm well aware of the damage it could do to all of us but especially to Charlie. I've been thinking about this every day and I think Grandpa's plan will work.'

'Whatever you want to do, I'll go along with it.'

'Good. There's no way he can prove that we ever slept together. As long as John and Charlie are never seen side by side nobody will believe him. I'll deny it and it's my word against his.'

'In which case, darling, there's no need for you to say anything to the boys. They can come back and tell us what he said and we can be equally shocked that he could have made up such a scandalous and damaging story.'

'The only flaw in this idea is that they will see John and then come straight back and see Charlie and might notice the resemblance.'

'Hang on, isn't there a photograph of you and John somewhere? Would you mind getting it and also bring over the snap you took on his birthday that's on your dressing table?'

She vanished into the walk-in wardrobe and reappeared with a shoebox. 'I think it's in here somewhere. You look for that and I'll go and get the photograph of Charlie, Julia and me.'

He rummaged through and found the one they were looking for. He prayed that his feeling about this was correct.

'Here you are – why did you want it?'

He held the two images together and laughed. 'Look, Charlie looks nothing like John now. In fact, he's the image of you but has fair hair.'

She picked them up and took them over to the brighter light in the centre of the room. When she turned to face him, her smile was blinding.

'You're right. I don't know why I didn't realise that myself. Hopefully, the boys will simply think it's sad that John's trying to destroy our lives because his own is so miserable.'

Alex reached out and put the tray back on his lap. He shared the sandwiches and apple pie with her and began to think that maybe once this John business was out of the way he was in with a chance of winning her back.

* * *

Babs found it difficult pretending everything was normal over breakfast the following morning. She was waiting to see if one of her brothers would bring up the meeting with John that afternoon. Neither of them mentioned it and she began to think they might have forgotten. Then as they slung their schoolbags over their shoulders and prepared to leave, Tom finally mentioned it.

'Don't forget, Babs, we're meeting John after school so we'll be back later than usual. Will be good to see him again but we're both mystified as to why he needs to come all the way from Hastings in order to tell us this piece of information in person.'

'I'm as puzzled as you are, Tom. Mrs B is doing a salad tonight so it doesn't matter when you come home.'

An ancient, but remarkably fit lady from the village came in twice a week to do the laundry and today Babs had the unenviable task of collecting and sorting the entire family's clothes before she arrived tomorrow morning. Mrs B still did the ironing as she said she found it relaxing. Babs now walked into the village to do the shopping, not that there was much available. Thank goodness they grew all their own vegetables and had eggs and chickens to eat.

Charlie had vanished upstairs to spend time with Alex and she put Julia in the pram and wheeled her into the sunshine so she could watch the fringes on the sun canopy blowing in the breeze. The sun was out but it was quite cool. The baby was well wrapped up and the fresh air would do her good.

Alex was playing snakes and ladders with Charlie when she went in to collect the things from the laundry bin in that room.

'Mummy, I've not been down any snakes at all but my daddy has.'

'That's good, darling. I hope you win.' She looked at Alex and he nodded. 'Julia's asleep in her pram in the garden and I'm on laundry collection. Will you two be all right for half an hour?'

'Absolutely spiffing, Babs. I can't tell you how much I'm enjoying being out of bed. I'm going to get dressed tomorrow whatever Edward says.'

'Why aren't I called Edward like Grandpa?'

She heard Alex answering as she dashed into her own room to collect her dirty clothes. The baby's things were already downstairs. Nappies were washed every day and she did those herself – it would hardly be fair to leave a week's worth of smelly cotton squares for anyone else to do.

The blackouts had been removed – there was now only a dim-out – and her grandparents had started to sit in the original, very grand drawing room. It appeared that as long as no actual lights were put on in the cavernous, glass-ceilinged rotunda they could now use all the other rooms and go up and down the main staircase.

The backstairs were more convenient to get to the kitchen. When she'd been pregnant she'd longed to use the main stairs again, but now she thought she'd continue to use the backstairs most of the time. The front of the house, which had been out of action for years, was slowly being brought back to life. She remembered when she'd arrived five years ago, before the war had really got started, Grandma had insisted they change for dinner.

There was no point in inviting people over for drinks, for dinner, for anything really, as there wasn't anything to give them apart from weak tea and boiled eggs. When would they ever have sufficient butter to make a decent cake?

With Julia in her arms she collected Charlie who'd spent a happy two hours playing board games with his daddy.

'Shall we go down the big stairs?'

'Yes, yes, I'm a big boy so I should use big stairs.'

He had scarcely been in the main part of the house as everyone lived in the guest wing. She wondered if Grandma would want to move back. There was a desperate shortage of fuel and they were now almost out of timber from the woodland. It didn't make sense to her to open up the house if they wouldn't be able to heat it. Better to keep things as they were until rationing ended – God knows when that would be.

Mrs B had taken the tray into the drawing room so she would have her tea with them. They rarely had coffee in the house and no one drank the horrible chicory and acorn mixture that was supposed to be coffee any longer. Charlie ran ahead.

'There you are, my dear girl. We thought you weren't going to join us.'

'I don't like to hurry when I'm carrying the baby as she's started trying to throw herself out of my arms and I have to hold her tight.'

'Put her down on the rug with Charlie, Babs, and sit with us for a little while. I expect you're anxious about the meeting this afternoon.'

They had to talk in code as her son picked up on everything.

'I'm sure it'll be fine.'

'What will be fine, Mummy?'

'Your uncles are meeting an old friend before they come home this afternoon. I'm just worried they might be out when it gets dark as I don't like them riding their bicycles then.'

'It's ever so bright in the street now those lights are on, silly Mummy.'

'Quite right, young man – what a clever little chap you are,' Grandpa said.

The afternoon dragged by and all the adults were constantly looking at the clock. School came out at four o'clock so the boys would be meeting John about now. He hadn't specified a place so presumably he was going to wait outside the gates. As long as they didn't bring him back with them, because that would be an absolute disaster. But he'd have to stay the night somewhere. Too late to do anything about it now. She would be glad when today was over one way or another.

Five thirty was bath time. Charlie insisted on having his with Julia, which usually ended up with her soaking wet by the time they'd finished. Even though she was no longer sleeping in the bedroom with its own bathroom, she continued to use it for the children.

'I might not be dressed, but I can still help with this rigmarole, darling, if you'll allow me to.'

'If you can sit on the stool then I can hand Julia to you. That will make things so much easier.'

This was the first time both of them had been involved and although almost as wet as usual she'd really enjoyed having Alex there and so had the little ones.

Julia still had a bottle first thing in the morning and last thing at night and this was standing in a jug of hot water on the dressing table.

'Why don't you give it to her, Alex? That way I can get Charlie into his pyjamas.'

As she was leaving the bedroom she heard the back door bang and her brothers came in. Her stomach clenched. She looked back at Alex and he'd heard it too.

'Don't worry, it'll be fine.'

She smiled her thanks at his confidence and bustled Charlie into his bedroom. Her brothers were coming up the stairs. Surely they wouldn't burst in and blurt out what they'd been told? No one was supposed to know why John had come so they all had to pretend to be appalled when they heard.

* * *

Julia was asleep before Babs came so he put the baby into her cot. He could hear Babs reading to Charlie. He paused at the bottom of the nursery stairs and there was the sound of the boys moving about there. Supper had been delayed, but he wondered if anyone was going to want to eat it.

His stomach was churning. He'd never felt so nervous. He'd flown through flak, been shot down, tortured, almost died a couple of times and hadn't been scared. When Babs had said things had been easier for him he'd been furious, but now he finally understood what she'd meant.

Being emotionally involved with people made everything so much more difficult. He hovered outside Charlie's bedroom waiting for her to come out. Whatever John had told the boys they needed to face it together – to brazen it out – and hope the problem went away. It was a bloody dreadful thing to do to John...

Good God! He had to speak to her before the boys came down. They'd been looking at this arse upwards, had a skewed perception, but now he saw things clearly. She stepped out and he grabbed her hand and led her into the bedroom, hoping he'd have time to speak to her before Tom and David came down. There was something he had to do first as well as speak to her.

The two photographs were in the chest of drawers and he grabbed the one with Charlie in it.

'Babs, I'm going to hold this photograph next to me. Look at it closely.'

She frowned but then did as he asked. Slowly it dawned on her. 'He looks like you – I've been so convinced that he was John's that I never considered the possibility I was wrong. He's got my eyes, your nose and heaven knows where he gets his colouring from.'

She flung herself into his arms and they were laughing and crying together. Eventually they pulled apart. 'I don't give a bugger what Edward said, I'm going to get dressed and come down.'

'All right, there's something I've got to do, something I should have realised. My guilty conscience has stopped me seeing what's right in front of my nose.'

She rushed off and he dressed in double quick time. He rather thought the boys were lurking upstairs, unwilling to come down and share their unpalatable news with everyone.

'Alex, come in here a minute,' she called him quietly from Charlie's room.

'What is it?'

She was standing by the bed and shining her torch on the little boy's head. 'Look, there are red glints in his hair now. How could we both be so blind?'

'You're right, darling – that settles it. We need to talk to your grandparents immediately and revise what we're going to say.'

They went down the main staircase, which meant he could keep his arm around her. He loved Charlie, had always considered him his son, but now he knew he really was his actual father it was as if a weight had been lifted from his shoulders.

Edward and Elspeth were in the drawing room. He was pacing up and down and she was sitting on the edge of her chair. He knew exactly how they felt.

'Grandpa, Grandma, we've got the most amazing, wonderful news. Charlie is quite definitely Alex's son. He's even got red hair showing amongst the blond.' She handed Edward the photograph. 'Look at him and then look at Alex.'

'Of course he is your son, my boy. One of us really should have seen this before.'

'Tom and David are going to come down in a minute. They will know that we're all together now. I'm not sure what we should say,' Babs said.

'As the paternity question is no longer an issue it's up to you whether you want to discuss this with your brothers, my dear girl.'

'They are old enough to be told, I think – I'm hoping they'll understand why I did what I did. If you don't mind, Alex, I don't want to lie about it. I feel really sorry for John as I misled him. For the past four years he's believed he was a father and now we've got to tell him he's wrong.'

'I'll ring him when he gets home. You don't have to speak to him, darling. Better coming from me in the circumstances.'

She looked at each of them in turn. 'Then we're agreed?'

15

Tom and David appeared at the drawing room door, dithering, reluctant to enter.

'Come in, boys, we're eager to hear what John had to tell you that was so important,' Babs said with a smile.

'There's no easy way to say this, Babs, so I'll just come out with it. John said that Charlie is his child. That you tricked Alex into marrying you.'

'Good heavens, what a ridiculous thing to say. However, I can see why he might think so.' She gestured that they should sit down. She'd worked out exactly what to say to them and although it involved a small lie, she was happy with this one.

'I'm not comfortable discussing this with you, it's really none of your business, and I think John was very wrong to involve you. However, I'm going to tell you why he is under this ridiculous misapprehension.

'I agreed to become engaged to John but never with the intention of marrying him. He was always in love with me; I loved him but not like that. When he came to my room the night before he left to go to Canada to train, I couldn't send him away. Remember, his arrival that afternoon had saved my life and that coloured my decision.'

Alex was watching Tom and David carefully but they didn't seem at all shocked by this revelation, merely interested.

'I was invited to a New Year's Eve party two weeks later. There was absolutely no possibility that John could be Charlie's father because I had my monthlies before I became involved with Alex.'

The boys exchanged happy smiles. 'The poor bloke – I can see why he might be confused. Charlie looked a bit like him when he was little. We should have brought him back with us so he could see Alex and Charlie together. That would have settled the matter,' Tom said.

'I'm sure I don't have to ask you not to pass this information on to anyone else.' The boys nodded and their grandmother answered as if Babs hadn't spoken.

'I'm glad that you didn't bring him here. That would have been rather embarrassing for all of us.'

'Did John say why he wanted to tell you in person?' Alex asked.

'To be honest, he wasn't making a lot of sense. He wasn't the same John we used to know. He's lost a lot of weight, walks with a limp and doesn't look at all well.' Tom exchanged a glance with his brother. 'There's something else. He said he's leaving the farm to Charlie.'

'Don't worry about it, boys. I'll make sure he understands. I just hope he hasn't repeated this nonsense to his parents,' Alex said. 'Did he say how long he's staying in Brentwood?'

'He said he was catching a train to London tonight and staying there and then returning to Hastings tomorrow morning.'

'Then I'll ring him tomorrow afternoon.'

'Anyway, why are you downstairs and dressed, Alex? We thought you had to stay upstairs until next week,' David said.

'I wanted to hear why John had summoned you and I'm feeling tickety-boo. I'm also more than ready for my supper.'

He held out his hand and without hesitation she took it. The conversation over supper was lively, John's visit forgotten. Her brothers took it in turns to check on the children and then retired to their bedroom to complete that night's homework.

'Alex, I insist that you go up too,' Grandpa told him firmly. 'I understand why you felt the urge to come down, but it's too soon. I don't want another setback.'

'Neither do I, Edward. Shall we compromise? I'll spend the morning in bed but come down in the afternoon and for supper.'

'Agreed. I'm hoping that as soon as you're fit enough you and Babs will take the children over to your parents and get things sorted out.'

'I will. It's gone on long enough. If I don't do something about it then they're going to lose Ned as well as he's on the brink of asking to move in here.'

'We'd love to have him, but his place is with his parents. However, if he turns up with his suitcase then I won't turn him away,' Grandma said.

Babs made the cocoa as always; however, tonight she didn't stay to drink it in the drawing room but took it upstairs so she could talk to Alex.

He was stretched out on the double bed and she sat beside him on the chair. From the gleam in his eye she thought it unwise to put temptation in his way. She was now as eager as he to resume their lovemaking. Having the worry about Charlie permanently removed had made her see things differently.

Also, the fact that they no longer had to worry about her inadvertently becoming pregnant was a bonus. After what had happened last time she didn't want another child, but it had taken her this long to understand her views had changed.

'It never bothered me, darling, that we didn't think Charlie was mine. He's my son and always has been. It seems extraordinary now that neither of us even considered the possibility that John wasn't his father.'

'I was so consumed with guilt at having slept with two men in the space of two weeks that when I saw what I thought was a convincing resemblance to John I automatically believed it.' She jumped up and joined him on the bed. 'I can't tell you how sorry I am that I've caused all this misery for nothing.'

'Forget about it. I have. We've been through so much that I almost feel someone upstairs has given us this miracle as a reward.'

She settled against his good shoulder and he put his arm around her. 'I've never been completely sure that I believe in God. I'm an agnostic, not an atheist. But you're right – John has done us a favour by coming.'

'As our son's hair is beginning to turn red we'd have eventually realised the truth without his precipitating things. I must say your brothers took the news that their sister has a racy past remarkably well.'

'Jim's tragic death changed all of us. They both grew up, as did Ned, and I treat them like adults now even though Tom's a sixth former and David's fourteen – they're not grown-ups.' She wriggled round so she could see his face. 'This beastly war's going to be over before Tom's called up, isn't it?'

'I'm certain it is. On D-Day we hoped it would be over by Christmas, but Hitler's still refusing to capitulate. I shudder to think how many more people will die, civilians and servicemen, before that maniac accepts defeat.'

'Let's not talk about that. We've lost your brother and Joe but now everyone we care about is home safe. I don't think that one of those horrible doodlebugs will drop on us as we're far enough from London to be safe.'

'I've been meaning to talk to you about the future. As you know I intended to remain in the RAF – that was my career choice originally – but obviously now I can't. I have to find something worthwhile to do.'

'Funnily enough we were talking about exactly that just before you came back from hospital. What about going to university and studying law?'

'I'm not sure I'm cut out to be a lawyer. I know I don't want to be an accountant...'

She laughed. 'Exactly what I said. I think you'd look very dashing in a black gown and wig.'

'I was thinking that if my shoulder recovers sufficiently then I'll apply to the police force. I'd like to be a detective – that does appeal to me. I'm an outdoor sort of chap and wouldn't be happy shut up in an office all day.'

'Police? At least the uniform's blue and that would suit you. Seriously, though, Alex, wouldn't you have to start as a lowly constable and then work your way up?'

'I've no idea how it works but I'm prepared to do whatever's necessary. I wouldn't be a constable for long and my aim is to be a detective chief superintendent eventually.'

Something occurred to her and she sat up, her heart racing, unexpectedly enthusiastic about his proposed choice of career. 'If you apply now, before the war's over, I'm certain they'll snap you up and make you at least a sergeant immediately. They must be desperately short of men as I believe policemen were given the option to sign up or remain where they were.'

'That's settled then. Tomorrow I'll start looking into it. I'm not allowed to exercise my arm and shoulder until the wound's fully healed. Edward had to stick another couple of stitches in after my stupidity the other day.'

'You can still make enquiries. Shall we have a little party to properly celebrate your homecoming soon? There are still a few shots left in the Brownie and there's someone in the village who will develop and print the film. I want to have a family photograph to commemorate the occasion.'

* * *

Alex pushed the hair from Babs's face and kissed her. Nothing threatening – a gentle, loving gesture – and to his delight she responded. It didn't last long but it meant more than any other kiss they'd exchanged.

'Darling, does this mean what I hope it does? No pressure, but are you going to sleep with me again when I'm fit?'

'I certainly am. Knowing Charlie's your son in every possible way has changed everything – it shouldn't have, but it has.'

'You've been carrying the guilt, the worry that something might come between us, ruin the family, all these years. It's hardly surprising it's made a difference. It certainly has to me. I'm not looking forward to speaking to John tomorrow but once that's done you can forget about him. We can move on with our lives.'

'There's still the small problem of your family blaming Tom and me for Jim's death. Obviously, things will never be quite the same, but until your mother and sister can put their prejudices aside I can't be truly happy.'

'I know, but when I explain to them that not only will they have lost Jim, but they will lose me, Charlie and Julia, and almost certainly Ned as well, if they don't change their attitude, I think they'll come round.'

'Let's hope so. We've had one miracle today – maybe there'll be another one. I'd better go – neither of us will have any sleep if I don't.' She leant over and kissed him again and then slid from the bed and ran out.

He couldn't stop smiling. He had everything to look forward to and even if his own sister and parents weren't part of it, he had his own family now and that was more than enough.

* * *

Alex stayed in his room Saturday morning, but came down just before lunch.

'Ned, good man. I wanted to talk to you.'

'I can guess what it's about. Shall we have a wander outside?'

Charlie was dancing round his feet waving a piece of paper for his attention. He ruffled the little boy's hair. How could none of them have seen that his son's hair was turning red?

'Daddy, Daddy, I've drawn you a lovely picture. Look at it now.'

'Show me, sweetheart. Oh, it's absolutely splendid.' He said that without looking at it properly but now he stared in astonishment. 'You've got Mummy, me, Julia, and your uncles – clever boy.'

'I wanted to put Grandma and Grandpa and Ned and Mrs B but I didn't have room. I'm going to do another one right now.'

Ned grinned. 'He's obviously another Picasso. I'm quite sure that none of us could draw so well at his age.'

'There's no need to go outside. Let's go in the study and close the door. Charlie's said what I was thinking. He thinks of you as part of this family and he didn't include our mum and dad. I'm beginning to think it's too late to mend that particular rift.'

'I'm afraid it is, Alex. To be honest, I don't really think that Valerie ever got over her breakdown when her baby died a few years ago. She and Mum won't even let me talk about Babs, Tom, David or the children.'

'What about Dad? I don't understand why he hasn't put his foot down. Do they really want to miss out on Charlie and Julia?'

'It's not rational, I know, but they gave Dad an ultimatum. Either he went along with them or Mum would move out.'

'Sod me! I don't have time for this. I'm not even going to try and put things right. It's their loss.'

'I told them that I was going to move in here, that you would be my guardian in future, unless they changed their minds. Mum told me to pack and David and I are going over to collect my things.'

'This is a bloody mess. Jim would be so upset to know that his death had caused the family to fall apart. There's nothing we can do about it at the moment. We just have to hope, pray, that as they get used to Jim not being here they'll feel differently.'

Ned looked down, uncomfortable about something. 'I don't have to stay at school. I can get a job somewhere.'

'You won't. We'll pay your school fees, and anything else. I think we need to get this arrangement made legal. I'll ask Edward – he adopted Tom and David a few years ago and had some sort of interim deal until that went through.'

'To be honest, since I told them I didn't want to take over the farm things have been a bit frosty and that's without this nonsense with Babs. This was always my second home – what's another Everton amongst friends?'

Tom offered to go with them but Ned said it would make things worse. He took Charlie and the dogs for a walk to the woods; Julia was having her afternoon nap upstairs, so Alex had no excuse not to make that phone call.

'Do you think John will be home by now, Babs?'

'It only takes a couple of hours even with the trains as they are at the moment. I'm certain he will be. Do you want me to stay with you or shall I go away?'

'Stay. Just in case you need to speak to him as well to reinforce the information.'

She nodded and sat behind the desk watching as he asked the operator to connect him. He was about to give up. The operator had already told him she was still trying to connect him, when John picked up the receiver.

'It's Alex Everton. We need to talk, John.'

No answer. He was about to repeat himself when John replied.

'They needed to know the truth. I'm going to tell my parents today that they have a grandchild.'

'No, John, they don't. I'm sorry, but I can categorically state Charlie is my child and not yours, whatever you believe. His hair is now turning red and it's clear that he looks like a combination of myself and Babs.'

'She told me herself that Charlie was mine. Why would she say something like that?'

'When he was little he had your colouring, not mine, and because of what happened that night she was feeling guilty. She jumped to conclusions – as we all did – but as he's grown it's obvious he's an Everton through and through.'

There was a long silence before John said, 'I've got nothing to live for now.'

Babs heard this comment and snatched the phone from him. 'John, don't be so silly. You've got your whole life ahead of you. You're a young man. You'll meet someone and get married and have children of your own one day. Maggie might not have been the one for you, but there will be someone. It's time for you to stop living in a fantasy world where you and I are together and Charlie is our child.'

Alex was shocked at how harsh she was being. The man was obviously suicidal and talking to him like that might push him over the edge.

'I'm sorry. Things have been difficult. I'm in constant pain from my leg and I drink too much because of this. Until I see for myself that he's not mine I can't accept it. You could just be telling me this to get rid of me – and I wouldn't blame you.'

Alex reached over and took the phone back. 'John, I can assure you that we're not lying but I understand why you doubt what we're saying. It's not safe to bring Charlie to London so you'll have to come here.'

'I can't leave the farm again this week but could come next.'

'Then we look forward to seeing you. You'll stay here of course. Say nothing to your parents until you've seen him. It wouldn't be fair to raise their hopes and then have to disappoint them.'

There was the sound of paper rustling – presumably a diary of some sort – and then John was back. 'I can come next Wednesday, the fourth of October. If I catch the early train I'll be there by lunchtime. No need to collect me; I might be lame, but I can walk from the station.'

The line went dead. Babs was looking at Alex as if he had escaped from a lunatic asylum.

'Why did you invite him here? Heaven knows what he's going to say.'

'He's hurting, Babs, and he's a good bloke. He almost died fighting for this country and he deserves our sympathy. I'll make sure he doesn't do or say anything to upset you.'

'You can't be sure of that. Don't forget your brother's going to be here too. I really don't want him knowing about my indiscretion.'

'He won't care – he's one of the family now. Don't worry, darling. In a way this is the best solution. I know how much you cared for John when you were growing up and it would be a shame if all that was lost. Maybe, after this visit, you can stay in contact with him and his family. After all, you think of his parents as your aunt and uncle, don't you?'

She walked into his arms – well, one arm, really – and he hugged her. 'I love you, Babs, and you love me and that's all that matters.'

16

Babs spent the next few days reorganising sleeping arrangements. Ned and David now had the bedroom that adjoined the nursery upstairs. Tom moved downstairs and had the last room in the guest wing. She'd managed to persuade her grandparents that opening up the main part of the house wasn't sensible at the moment.

Alex was fully recovered, according to him, but Grandpa still insisted he took things easy. His arm was no longer in a sling and he was beginning to use it, although not as freely as he had before his injury.

The day before John was due to arrive it started to rain heavily. 'We can't let him walk from the station in this weather, Alex, but neither can we go in the pony cart,' she said.

'Don't worry about it, sweetheart – it might be fine again tomorrow. A more pressing problem is where do you intend that he sleeps?' His smile was wicked and she tingled all over.

'Oh, all right then, I'll move back in with you and John can have that room. Don't smile like the Cheshire cat, Squadron Leader Everton. Nothing is going to happen in bed apart from sleeping until my grandfather gives his permission.'

His laughter filled the room. 'I'll go and ask him right now. That should be an interesting conversation for both of us.'

She was about to call his bluff but decided this was something she really didn't wish to share with her grandparents. 'There's no need to bother him. What happens tonight depends...' She couldn't think of what it might depend upon.

Next thing she was in his arms and his kiss left her in no doubt that they would be making love. Breathless, she pushed him away. 'If you say anything about an early night in front of everyone I'll sleep with Charlie. I'm warning you, Alex.'

He smoothed back her hair, which had come loose in their passionate embrace. 'It's been literally months, darling, and until I can hold you naked in my arms, I won't believe that things are finally as they should be.'

'Daddy, why does Mummy want to take her clothes off to give you a cuddle?'

Charlie had wandered into the sitting room and overheard his last remark. She pressed her face into Alex's shoulder trying to stem her giggles. 'You can answer his question, and good luck with that.'

He cleared his throat. 'Erm... ah... well...'

She took pity on him. 'Charlie, you know it's rude to listen to other people's conversations. Come along, you can help me get Julia up from her nap.'

This was enough to distract her son and she walked away smiling. Alex still had a lot to learn about being a parent.

The talk over supper that night wasn't about the progress of the war. Grandpa had begun listening to the nine o'clock news every night again, but nobody else joined him. She always made a point of being upstairs with her cocoa by then.

'Ned and I have got news for you,' David said as they were eating their dessert of apple and pear crumble.

'What's that, young man? From your expression it's good news not bad,' Grandpa said.

'As far as we're concerned it's the best possible news.'

He went on to explain that as soon as they were sixteen they could apply to Sandhurst and for a medical bursary.

'Then eventually we'll have four doctors in the family,' Tom said happily.

'I think this an appropriate time to tell you all that I'm intending to join the police force – hopefully as a detective – as soon as I'm declared hundred per cent fit.'

'I know the chief constable, Alex. I'll speak to him if you like.'

'Thank you, Edward. I'd appreciate that.'

The boys vanished to do their homework as soon as the meal was over. Grandma, for once, didn't want to go to bed early but got out her embroidery frame. Grandpa had a pile of medical journals to read.

'We're going up now. Goodnight.' Alex stood up and held out his hand. With scarlet cheeks she took it and mumbled her own goodnights.

She was whisked through the door and she wasn't sure if she was pleased or cross that he'd been so blatant.

'Edward, I'm so happy that Alex and Babs are going to be together tonight. It's been far too long since they were estranged.'

'Let's hope he doesn't overdo it, my dear. Too much energetic activity might damage his shoulder again.'

Babs pressed her free hand over her mouth to hold back her giggles. Alex was biting his lip and they ran upstairs and burst into the bedroom where they could laugh without fear of being heard.

'I'm going to be so embarrassed tomorrow morning. Do you think they'll enquire as to how things went?'

'Probably.' He wiped his eyes. 'I'll check the children, darling. You can have the bathroom first.'

He was gone before she could respond. He'd not seen the scar that ran from her navel all the way down her stomach. It had healed well enough, was only a thin pink ridge now, but he might be horrified. Maybe it would be better to keep her nightdress on.

She stripped to her bra and knickers and cleaned her teeth. After a quick wash she removed the last items and slipped on her prettiest nightie. It was soft, white cotton lawn with hand-embroidered panels. She'd made it herself especially for tonight.

'Good, I won't be a minute. That's a lovely nightdress, darling, but you won't be needing it.' Alex smoothed his hand down her arm as he passed and his eyes were dark with passion. 'I won't be a minute.'

Her pulse was racing. It was as if electricity was running up and down her body. She couldn't bring herself to remove her nightgown and was about to scramble into bed when he emerged. He was naked, ready to make love, and he strode towards her. Seconds later she was as naked as he.

Whatever she'd been going to say about her scars was forgotten. They fell backwards onto the bed and her fears evaporated.

A considerable time later they were lying face to face, both flushed, both deliriously happy. 'It's like riding a bike – you don't forget how to do it.' She ran a finger down his cheek and he captured it in his mouth. A wave of heat engulfed her.

Eventually they slept and when she woke, she glanced at the clock. She shot up in the bed. 'Alex, it's ten o'clock. What about Julia? I...'

'The boys agreed to get the children up and then Mrs B and your grandparents are looking after them until we go down.'

'Horrible man. How could you involve my brothers in this?'

His arm encircled her waist and she was pulled back beneath the sheets. 'Don't be such a prude, darling. Sex is part of married life and nothing to be ashamed of.'

'And you've had quite enough of that for one day. I'm going to have a bath – no, on my own – and then I'm getting dressed and going to take care of my children. You can have the water after me.'

Reluctantly he released her. 'You're right. Too much energetic activity is bad for a recovering hero.'

She snatched a pillow and hit him with it and then skipped into the bathroom. She could hear him laughing as she pushed the bolt across, just in case he had other ideas.

* * *

In fact, Alex didn't have the energy to continue their passionate lovemaking and was grateful to have half an hour to relax and gather his thoughts. It hardly seemed possible that a few weeks ago he was risking his life several times a day flying sorties with his squadron.

They'd lived and fought together for months and yet he'd not given them a thought since he'd been back. He was one of the lucky ones, had survived when so many hadn't. And look at that poor bastard, John, who'd crashed in his bomber, barely survived and was now damaged physically and mentally – possibly permanently disabled.

The sheets needed changing – he could do that for Babs whilst she bathed. Not only had he remade the bed, but he'd also laid out both his clothes and hers. He wondered if she'd agree to wear what he'd selected for her. Flannels, a crisply ironed shirt and a blazer for him and a pretty nip-waisted frock with a floral pattern in shades of pink and blue for her.

The door opened and clouds of steam drifted into the bedroom. She emerged pink-cheeked and wrapped only in a towel.

'I thought you'd drowned in there you've been so long.' He kissed her as he walked past and she smelt like roses – infinitely desirable. 'Good grief, it's like a jungle in here. There's certainly more than the regulation five inches in that bath.'

'I'm afraid the mirror's too steamed up for you to shave at the moment but if you leave the door open it will probably clear.'

You could almost swim in the giant bath and he revelled in the luxury of having so much water he could actually submerge himself. A bit of a waste that they hadn't shared it.

When he reappeared to get dressed the clothes on the bed were gone and so was she, but they could be back in the wardrobe and not on Babs. He didn't have time to check. John could be here soon and they still hadn't had breakfast. His son was halfway up the stairs obviously looking for him.

'It's not raining today, Daddy, so will you come outside and play cricket with me?'

'Not today, Charlie, we've got a guest coming. I'll definitely play with you tomorrow if it's fine.'

'Why are you and my mummy up so late? Were you feeling poorly?'

'Not at all, but I'm certainly hungry. Do you think there's any bread left so you can make me some toast?' Avoiding awkward questions was going to become second nature to him soon.

* * *

Everyone – apart from the boys, who were out – had made an effort to look smart for this visit. Even the children had on their best outfits. They gathered in the drawing room at noon. No one was looking forward to John coming and he hoped that the bloke didn't react badly.

He was delighted that Babs was wearing the frock he'd chosen. They sat together on the sofa and Charlie was on the rug with Julia, building towers that she knocked down whilst squealing with laughter.

'Will he come to the front door or go round to the back?' Alex asked.

'Mrs B will answer whichever one he appears at, Alex,' Elspeth said.

'I'll answer the door, Grandma. Mrs B has more than enough to do preparing lunch for all of us.' Babs smiled at the old lady to take the sting from her words.

There was a palpable atmosphere in the drawing room. Why the hell were they so nervous when you only had to look at Charlie to see he was an Everton? He leant down and stroked the boy's floppy red-gold hair.

'It's as if his hair has turned red overnight, my boy. How could we be so unobservant?' Edward straightened his tie – it was the fourth time he'd done it in the past ten minutes.

'I know. Ridiculous isn't it?' He grinned at Babs. 'We're sitting here like a row of stuffed dummies in our Sunday best – that's even more ridiculous. It's not the vicar coming to tea.'

'The vicar?' Elspeth echoed. 'I didn't know we were expecting him today. We don't have any cake or scones.'

Edward leant over and patted her hand. 'It's John coming, my love, and he won't care if there's no cake or scones, I'm sure.'

Alex exchanged a glance with Babs. Elspeth wasn't herself and Babs would soon have to accept the inevitable decline.

From where she was sitting she could see the drive and he thought that deliberate. 'Our guest is coming, Charlie. Do you want to come with me to welcome him?'

Alex was about to suggest this was a bad idea but Edward shook his head. Maybe it would be better for John to see Charlie alone.

He scooped up the baby and handed her to Babs. 'Take Julia as well, darling.'

She nodded. There was no doubting the parentage of either child when they were seen so close together. He moved to a position by the window where he could see out but not be seen himself. He wanted to observe this crucial first meeting.

Babs had taken the children out through the back door and a few minutes later she appeared with Charlie trotting along beside her – chatting away as always – and she walked briskly towards the approaching figure.

The boys were right: the man limping towards the house didn't look well. He thought John might be a year or two older than him but at the moment he looked ten years older.

Babs had obviously called out. He couldn't hear from inside, but John's reaction made it clear. The man stopped and straightened. He stared at Charlie first, then turned his attention to Julia and Babs.

To Alex's astonishment instead of looking dejected John smiled and held out his hand to Babs who hurried forward and grasped it.

'Everything's tickety-boo, folks. For some reason John seems pleased that Charlie's not his son. I'm going out to join them.'

The front door hadn't been opened for years but the bolt slid back smoothly and the key turned in the lock. He pulled open the door and bounded down the steps.

'Hello, welcome. I'm Alex and you, of course, are John.' He walked forward with his hand outstretched and without hesitation the man shook it vigorously.

'Thank you for inviting me. I don't deserve to be welcomed so warmly after what I've put you through. You've got two wonderful children, Alex, and I envy you.'

Charlie was dancing around eager to join in the conversation. 'I'm Charlie Everton. Are you a friend of my mummy and my daddy?'

John leant down and offered his hand as if to an adult. 'How do you do, Master Everton. I'm John Thorogood and delighted to meet you.'

The little boy shook hands enthusiastically. 'I'm four years old. This is my baby sister, Julia. She's not even a year old yet.'

Alex put his arm around Babs's shoulders. No harm in showing their guest that Babs was his wife and happy to be so.

* * *

John had had plenty of time to get used to the possibility that the little boy he'd always thought of as being his own was nothing of the kind. There'd been no real necessity for him to visit in order to confirm this, but he'd really wanted to see Babs again. Not for any other reason than that she'd always been his best friend and he really needed one now.

When he'd looked up at her call and seen both children, the baby with a shock of red hair and the little boy with a mix of red and gold, he'd been relieved, not disappointed.

They entered through the imposing front door and into the spectacular rotunda through which the sunlight streamed. He shook hands with Dr Sinclair and his wife and they were equally friendly.

'Thank you for inviting me to stay, Mrs Sinclair.'

'I'm delighted to see you again, Mr Thorogood. You were always a very good friend to our granddaughter.'

Charlie tugged at his trouser leg. 'Do you play cricket, Uncle John? My daddy says he'll play too if it's not raining tomorrow.'

'I used to, but I hurt my leg when my aeroplane crashed and I don't run about much any more.'

'My daddy was blown up by a piece of cake and he had to come home.'

Over an informal lunch the full story was explained and for the first time in years he was able to laugh and talk as if he was a normal sort of bloke, not a cripple with a drink problem.

Alex took the baby up for an afternoon sleep and Charlie went with him. The grandparents had also retired, leaving him alone with Babs.

'Look, I don't know where to start. I've behaved like an absolute brute...'

'We don't blame you. It's as much our fault as yours for misleading you. I was so convinced that Charlie was yours that none of us noticed how much he'd changed since he was a toddler. I should never have got engaged to you and certainly not have slept with you. If I hadn't done that all our lives would have been so much easier.'

'I didn't tell my parents. I never intended to. I just wanted to see you again. I'd like to be friends if you can forgive me.'

'Nothing to forgive.' She smiled at him and he laughed.

'I've carried your image in my heart for years, convincing myself that I still loved you, but the girl I was in love with doesn't exist. We've both changed. Now – we've got a lot of catching up to do. Tell me what's been happening in your life and I'll do the same.'

Alex wandered in and flopped down in a chair and joined in the conversation. Every ten minutes or so one or other of them got up, presumably to check both children were sleeping safely, and then returned. He thought it odd that Alex was so involved with the children but the bloke had nothing else to do now so it made a sort of sense.

He couldn't remember the last time he'd enjoyed himself so much. This time, when Babs left the room she didn't come back, leaving him alone with Alex.

The talk turned to things better not discussed in front of those who hadn't been involved. Mrs B brought in a tray of tea but nobody else disturbed them.

'What time do the boys get back?'

'I don't know if Babs told you, but my younger brother now lives here permanently. They cycle from Brentwood and usually get here just before five o'clock. Bloody hell – it's a quarter to. The children will be having their tea soon. Care to join us in the kitchen?'

'I certainly would. Babs was right to tell me to pull myself together and stop living in a fantasy. I want what you've both got – a happy family. I don't suppose you know any young ladies you could introduce me to?'

'Can't help you there, my friend. I'd have thought there must be other suitable candidates as you've got the Land Army working on your farm. What about Maggie?'

'No, sadly I treated her very badly. I think I only proposed to her because she looks a little like Babs. But you're right, I'm sure there's someone for me. You'll be relieved to know that I'm no longer in love with your wife.'

'About time you gave up on her. How long can you stay? It's good to talk to someone who understands what I've been through. I've not told Babs the truth about anything really.'

'I can stay as long as you'll have me. Are you sure that Babs will be happy for me to be here more than one night? What about the boys? They certainly made it clear what they thought of me the other week.'

'They're pragmatic young men. When Jim died it changed everything and all three of them grew up in a hurry.'

17

John's visit had gone spectacularly well, Babs decided. When he'd left on the Friday they were all sorry to see him go and he promised to come again, but was rather vague as to when that might be. Her grandparents using the main drawing room again meant the sitting room was free for herself and Alex. The drawing room would have to be closed again when the weather got worse but at least, for a few weeks, they had the semblance of a private family life.

'I didn't realise how much I missed talking shop with a fellow pilot. John and I have got a lot in common even without the fact that we've both been in love with the same woman.'

'If you'd said anything else I would have punched you.' She put down the small frock she was smocking for Julia in order to throw a cushion at him. He caught it with the hand of his injured side and laughed at her. 'John seemed happier when he left, don't you think?'

'I agree and was puzzled that he didn't commit to another trip here. He wasn't just putting on a brave face – I'm certain of it.' Alex tossed the cushion back so it landed neatly beside her.

'So am I. On another subject entirely do you think that

Grandma is becoming vaguer, not following conversations as well or remembering things like she used to?'

'I spoke to Edward about it only this morning,' Alex said. 'He's remarkably philosophical. Doesn't seem bothered and says that her decline is going to be gradual. Nothing we can't manage between us.'

'Well, as he was always telling me when I first arrived here five years ago, he's a medical man and knows what he's talking about.' She resumed her sewing and Alex picked up his book, a murder mystery written by Agatha Christie.

'Another thing that's changing, sweetheart, is that Charlie isn't going to agree to an afternoon rest for much longer. Also, when I went in to Julia this morning she was trying to pull herself up on the cot bars. I think she's going to be walking before she's a year old.'

'I'm so happy you're taking such an interest in our children. I can't believe any other husband is quite so interested. You really don't have to change nappies, do so much, if you don't want to.'

'Of course I want to. I wouldn't do it if I didn't. By the way, I've got an interview next week with the chief constable, did I tell you?'

'You didn't. I'm still not convinced it's the right career for you – from what Grandpa was saying you only get promoted if you fit in, agree with everything your superiors say, and follow the rules completely. I can't see you keeping quiet if you see something that you don't agree with.'

'True enough. It's just an interview, Babs. I'm not committing myself to anything.'

Charlie appeared at the door. 'You're not listening, Mummy and Daddy. My baby sister's crying and she's done a poo in her nappy.'

'Oh dear, no wonder she's upset. You stay with your daddy. I'll go and sort her out. I thought we could go for a walk to the village before tea. What do you think, Charlie?'

'Can we go in the cart? It's lovely and bumpy in the back of that and Silver would like to come out with us.'

'I don't see why not. I won't be long.'

She was already wearing warm slacks and a pretty coral twinset that had been an unexpected gift from her grandparents. It had belonged to Grandma but had never been worn.

When she returned with the wriggling baby in her arms the sitting room was empty. She checked in the boot room and saw that her son and husband had on their coats and shoes so must already be outside.

'Come along, baby, your daddy and brother are in the stables waiting for me to harness Silver.'

'Dada, Dada.' Julia clapped her hands and repeated it several more times. Seven months was early for a baby to start talking but Babs was sure her daughter had definitely been talking about Alex.

To her surprise when she reached the stable yard her mare was already in the shafts and the cart waiting to go. Before she could comment the baby tried to launch herself at Alex.

'Dada, Dada.' Julia held out her arms making it quite clear she was actually addressing him.

'Well, little one, I didn't know you could speak. What a clever girl you are.' He took her and held her up in the air whilst she squealed in delight.

Charlie was already in the cart but turned to watch. 'She's clever. She can already say my name. She said it first.'

'Can she? I've not heard her – what does she call you?' Babs asked as she was checking the buckles and straps were correctly done up.

'She calls me Lee Lee. Now she can say my daddy's name too but she doesn't say yours, does she, Mummy?'

'I'm sure she will soon.'

Alex was sitting on the rear seat with the baby on his lap and

Charlie on his other side. As the driver, she took the front seat, unhitched the reins, released the brake and clicked her tongue.

She followed the well-used track that ran around the estate and through the woods. There was sufficient room to turn the vehicle in a small glade in the centre of the trees.

'Charlie, do you want to hold the reins?'

'I do, I do.'

The little boy scrambled over the back of the seat and landed with a thud beside her. Immediately Julia started to wail. 'Lee Lee, Lee Lee.' No doubting that the baby was definitely talking.

The round trip took over an hour and the sun was setting as they trotted into the yard. Tom was waiting to help.

'David and Ned aren't back from visiting friends in the village, Babs, but they'll be here in time for supper.'

'Uncle Tom, Julia can say my name and my daddy's name but she can't say Mummy at all.'

'I didn't know she could say anything. Let me help you down, Charlie. It's a long way to fall.'

***

It wasn't until they were getting ready for bed that she had an opportunity to speak to Alex about something dreadful that he didn't appear to have noticed himself. Before she did, she thought she'd test her theory just to be sure.

He'd removed his shirt and vest and was about to unbutton his trousers. She was standing next to him in her underwear. Suddenly she pretended to lose her balance. He reacted exactly as she'd expected. His right arm shot out and he caught her easily.

'I knew it, and now I'm certain. Your arm's working perfectly.'

He smiled and lifted her into the air. 'I was wondering when you were going to comment. There was no need for that charade, darling. You know what this means, don't you?'

'I'm afraid I do. You're going to re-enlist, aren't you?'

'I don't have any choice. I'm an experienced flyer. If they need me then I have to go.'

* * *

Alex had been dreading telling Babs he'd regained full use of his arm and was quite capable of flying a Spitfire or a Typhoon.

'The interview next week – it's not with any chief constable, is it?'

'No, it isn't. I wasn't going to tell you until I knew for certain I was fit for duty.'

'You've done your bit; nobody would know that your shoulder's fully recovered. You could stay here and be safe. The war's almost over.'

'I know. I'm surprised you haven't asked about any of this, Babs. I've not actually been discharged. I'm still officially on sick leave, waiting to be demobbed. The interview is actually with the medic at Hornchurch.'

She was pressing herself against him, making it hard to concentrate on anything but his desire.

'I don't want you to go, but I won't stop you. We've had these wonderful weeks together so I must be grateful for that. Will you promise me one thing?'

'If I can. What is it?'

'Ask if you can stay at Hornchurch – fly Spitfires again – not go to France and fly those horrible fighter-bombers.'

He was about to tell her that actually it was safer flying one of those than it was a Spit but thought better of it. She just wanted him close enough to come home occasionally.

'I'll ask, but I have to follow orders. I'd much rather be based somewhere familiar and be able to see you all occasionally.'

She pulled his head down and kissed him fiercely. They fell backwards onto the bed and made passionate love.

Eventually he was able to talk again. 'That's the first time we've made love when I had my socks on.'

She giggled. 'And it had better be the last. Mind you, at one point I thought you might still have your trousers and underpants on too.'

'I'm sorry, darling, but there was always a faint possibility this would happen. It won't be as bad before, as we know it won't be for much longer.'

Now was not the time to tell her that he would probably be flying sorties over the front line every day in support of the advancing troops.

* * *

It seemed odd putting on his uniform and when Charlie saw him he refused to talk and ran away and hid in his toy cupboard. His son understood that him dressing like this meant that his daddy would be going away.

'Good luck, darling. I know you really want to be fit again so you can resume your career.'

'Thank you, sweetheart. I love you, but this is who I am. I'd feel like a deserter if I didn't do this.'

Turning up at Hornchurch was like coming home. He was recognised at the gate and waved through without having to identify himself. He marched briskly to the admin block and from there to see the doc. The examination was thorough and he got the result he'd hoped for. He headed back to speak to the man who would soon be his CO.

* * *

Babs kept busy all day. Mrs B agreed to keep an ear out for Julia whilst the baby slept and her grandparents were entertaining Charlie in the drawing room. This gave her the opportunity to exercise both horses.

Bruno, the massive bay gelding, flew over the hedges and ditches and was an exhilarating ride. However, she still preferred her little mare who could jump just as far and travel even faster. By the time she'd finished brushing down Silver, two hours had passed.

Guiltily she ran in knowing that Julia would probably be awake and it wasn't fair on Mrs B to have to look after her baby as well as do everything else.

The kitchen was empty but she could hear Charlie talking to someone upstairs. Alex was back – they must have let him come home to collect his kit, which had arrived the week after him.

She rushed upstairs and found him sitting on the floor in Charlie's bedroom with Julia between his legs and Charlie on his knee. He wasn't in uniform.

'They don't want me, Babs. I've been officially demobbed.'

She dropped down beside him, her heart hammering, hardly able to believe what she'd heard. 'Is your shoulder not fully mended then?'

'It is. I'm fighting fit but surplus to requirements. I don't have to be a policeman – I'm going to apply immediately to be a commercial pilot. I have a better chance of being accepted whilst the war's still going on.' He kissed away her tears and for once Charlie didn't comment. 'It's over. I'm home for good and life just couldn't be any better.'

Barbara closed her eyes for a second, too overwhelmed to speak. The war was over for her family, her beloved Alex was no longer in danger and they now had the rest of their lives to enjoy the children and make plans together as a family.

They were the lucky ones and she sent up small prayer of thanks to whoever might be listening. It certainly seemed like a miracle that her life had eventually turned out so well.

ABOUT THE AUTHOR

Fenella J. Miller is a bestselling writer of historical sagas. She also has a passion for Regency romantic adventures and has published over fifty to great acclaim.

Sign up to Fenella J. Miller's mailing list for news, competitions and updates on future books.

Visit Fenella's website: www.fenellajmiller.co.uk

Follow Fenella on social media here:

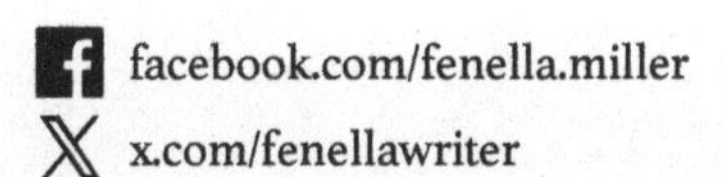

facebook.com/fenella.miller
x.com/fenellawriter

ALSO BY FENELLA MILLER

Goodwill House Series

The War Girls of Goodwill House

New Recruits at Goodwill House

Duty Calls at Goodwill House

The Land Girls of Goodwill House

A Wartime Reunion at Goodwill House

Wedding Bells at Goodwill House

A Christmas Baby at Goodwill House

The Army Girls Series

Army Girls Reporting For Duty

The Pilot's Girl Series

The Pilot's Girl

A Wedding for the Pilot's Girl

A Dilemma for the Pilot's Girl

A Second Chance for the Pilot's Girl

Standalone

The Land Girl's Secret

Milton Keynes UK
Ingram Content Group UK Ltd.
UKHW041314270324
440251UK00012B/97

9 781835 186534